DROWNING IN A HITTA'S LOVE

SWEET TEE

MZ. LADY P PRESENTS, LLC

ACKNOWLEDGMENTS

I am grateful for all of the opportunities that have come my way. I continue to pray for many blessings to fall in my lap. Thank you to my supporters and readers. Thank you for reading my work, sharing a link, or suggesting my book to someone. Special thanks to my mentors who I will not name for the continuous support and encouragement.

Thank you, Boss Lady, aka, Patrice Williams, better known as National Best Selling Author, Mz. Lady P. You have guided, encouraged, and never given up on me, and I appreciate it. For two years, I have learned so much as an author from you on how to promote and brand myself. Your hard work and dedication do not go unnoticed, nor do I take you for granted. I look forward to growing and becoming the dopiest author I can be under your company. You are stuck with me FOREVER! LOL. You are a beast in this industry, so to be a part of your team is a wonderful feeling. Thank you for seeing the potential in me during a difficult time in my life.

Shout out to my dope pen sisters. Our family is growing and glowing with talent across the board. I'm proud of you all. Thank you for always keeping it real and for providing advice and motivation. This is book # 9 y'all! It's an amazing feeling to add to my book collection. I want to thank my mother as she watches from heaven and continues to give me inspiration. There is not one day that goes by that I do not think about you. You inspire some of my crazy characters from the stories that you used to share about back in the day. Continue to watch over your son and me.

To those who have a dream, follow it and never give up! Push through, and if you want it bad enough, your hard work will pay off. The stories I write always have some type of message to it, and it is my sincere hope that it inspires the readers. Living the life we were dealt is easier said than done for some folks. Therefore, it is nice to get lost in others' drama via a good book. Each character created is based on friends, old associates, and from people watching.

Lastly, I would like to acknowledge myself for fighting against depression. Each day is a challenge, especially during November and December. The loss of a mother is a hard pill to swallow. Depression can consume and turn you into a different person unless you fight it! I write to cope, I write to inspire, and I write to promote my story.

Love yours truly,
~Sweet Tee

KEEP UP WITH SWEET TEE

SYNOPSIS

Have you ever met someone that took your breath away or made your heart skip a beat? Someone who went from stranger to best friend? Erika Cain found that and more in Tyree Lyons. A chance encounter leads them to cross paths and form a bond. What was initially like two ships passing in the night became a unique friendship between the two that will endure many tests over the course of their love affair. Tyree Lyons, a man of few words, never showed emotion no matter the situation. Raised in foster care, he learned early that love didn't love anybody, and it was a dog eat dog world. When he met Erika, his life changed forever. Like yin and yang, Tyree and Ericka became inseparable, giving a new meaning to opposites attract.

With all good things comes strife. Both Tyree and Ericka are about to embark on a journey that will test their strength, faith, and the love they have for one another. A life-threatening event will put things into perspective for Ericka. Everything she once knew and understood about love becomes questionable. She's drowning in a hitta's love and has no idea what to do, especially when the heart becomes torn between the two.

PROLOGUE

TYREE LYONS

"ERIKA, I'M BACK, BABY!" I shouted as I entered the door. The sounds of water running led me upstairs to her bedroom. I entered the steamy bathroom, careful not to scare her ass to death. "Hey, baby," I announced.

"Shit!" she exclaimed. I heard the sound of her bar soap when it dropped.

I let the toilet seat cover down and took a seat while I watched her silhouette through the glass shower doors. When she finished and turned off the water, the opaque color faded, leaving the glass clear again. Erika stood in her birthday suit, gracing my eyes with all of her beauty. Perfect in every way, I was a lucky muthafucka to hook up with her. I began to cheese hard as hell until she hesitantly faced me exiting the shower.

"What the fuck happened to yo' face, Erika? Answer me now!" I shouted.

"Bishop slapped me. He—" I cut her off from speaking.

"That punk ass nigga put his hands on you? Oh, hell naw, that shit is not riding at all! Go get dressed right now, we about to go teach his ass a lesson on respecting women."

When Erika turned around, and I saw her face, I wanted to kill somebody before knowing what even happened. Her bruised face made it difficult for me to look at her. She tried her best to hide it from me, but it was impossible to miss. When she said that bitch ass nigga's name, the bounty on his head went from twenty thousand dollars to a free kill. There was no way he would live after what he did.

I made Erika get dressed, and we drove to Bishop's house for revenge. Bishop was on my hit list. Whatever the reason wasn't my concern. I was paid to kill with no questions asked. However, his recent actions of putting his hands on my woman gave me a reason to murk him. As a professional, I did a few stakeouts to learn his routines, habits, and entrances to his house.

I pulled over and parked on the side street as I shut off my lights and turned off the engine. The neighborhood was dead with no activity, almost like a dark Halloween night after the kids were in bed. I turned to Erika, who showed no emotion.

"Baby, you okay? You ready to do this shit?"

Without a word, she shook her head up and down as the dark hoodie she wore covered her face. It is evident that she was still embarrassed, but that shit would heal up. I tried to make her feel better as I leaned over to kiss her.

"I love you, E. Don't ever forget that shit either. We about to go fuck this nigga up then we can go home and cuddle while I stroke your hair. Let's be smart and careful because what's about to happen could get both our asses arrested. If you think you can't do this, let me know now."

"I can do it! What's our plan?"

"You go to the front door and get him to let you inside while I creep in through the back entrance. He won't expect me at all because his focus will be on you the entire time. My goal is to kill him quickly after we smack him around for a bit," I detailed.

"Alright, let's do this," she responded.

I popped the trunk as we exited the vehicle, continuously checking our surroundings. I reached in and unzipped the black duffle bag filled with latex gloves, barbwire, switchblades, and all types of gadgets. I slipped on a black baseball cap and loaded up, ready to do what I did best.

"Here," I handed her a disposable pair of black shoe covers. She looked at me funny.

"Grab two pair of gloves, and put a pair in each pocket. Remember don't touch anything unless you have on gloves," I demanded while I tucked Thelma in the back of my pants and the silencer in my right front pocket.

"Okay. Damn, we on some Bonnie and Clyde type of ish," she commented with a smirk.

It was now or never, so we made our move as we began to carry out the plan we agreed on in the car. The two-story modern home was too big for one person to live in, I thought while walking closer to it. Erika walked along the walkway up to the front cherry wood door. With my gloves on, I swiftly approached the back area of the home, not expecting my task to be an easy one.

I pulled my tools out to pick the lock but decided to try something first. With a simple twist of the doorknob, I pushed a little, and it opened. It amazed me how many folks didn't lock their doors. Upon entering cautiously, I tucked my tools back into my pocket. Bishop lived alone, which made shit easy. Cool as a cucumber it didn't take long before I was able to follow the sound of Erika's voice.

Before busting in the living room, I listened a little longer. Bishop confessed he loved her and how he didn't mean to hit her. He explained how the call from his sister caused him to react and strike her. Erika began to cuss him out using every profanity word she could think of. Not trying to hear his excuse, I pulled my pistol out and made my appearance known. My entrance made Erika move quickly out of reaching distance.

"What up, nigga? I heard you like to put your hands on women. I hope you know yo ass is grass." Caught off guard his instinct to make a move for his pistol failed. Erika beat him as she removed it from inside a drawer. It was a nice Super Carry .45 ACP, and my baby looked good holding it too.

"Erika, hit his ass hard as you possibly can!" I yelled as I instructed her. It took her minute, but then she slapped the fuck out of him.

"It's sad to see you on your knees in a manner that isn't enjoyable. You should have more respect for females. The time we spent together was fun, but I always belonged to this crazy ass man right here," Erika taunted.

Bishop yelled, "Y'all won't get away with this shit, on my life! My boy Chico will come for you, bitch!"

Whoop!

I hit his ass again for disrespecting my girl. That nigga didn't have manners even in the last minutes of his life. As I stood over his body, ready to send him to his maker, he raised his head to say his final words.

"Erika, let me confess one last thing before—" was the last thing Bishop said before I put a bullet in his head. His body fell on the hardwood floor.

"Aye, enough of this shit, baby. Let's finish so we can go home."

"Okay, do you know where he keeps valuables and shit so we can make it look like a robbery? Make sure to change gloves again. There can be no trace of we were here. What about enemies or anyone with a grudge?"

"Shit, he had some cash and jewelry in a safe upstairs, but I never found out about the locations of his other monies. His boy Chico might suspect me because of an altercation he witnessed between us."

"What? Never mind, we will talk about that in the car, but right now we need to clean up and got out of dodge ASAP."

Erika led the way upstairs to his bedroom without touching anything but the big off gray combination safe. I kept an eye on my watch while she worked. We couldn't afford getting caught. I usually did shit like this solo. With a few twists left and right, it opened.

"It took me two weeks to learn the code numbers 27-15-37. I had to listen to his stories about life and family. Eventually, I read between the lines."

"I knew you would come through, baby."

My queen was a rider who had my respect and loyalty. Any female who had the balls to do the type of shit she did was truly a down ass chick. What happened next made the relationship between Erika and me stronger than ever. She was forever my down ass bitch. That night forever changed us both to the extent that death was the only way out of this relationship. She knew too much of my business and vice versa, which made us both liable to each other's downfall if it ever came to that point. From the house to the car, we made it home without incident. I was ready for pussy, a shower, and sleep in whatever order it came.

⸺

We stood together in the large walk-in shower as the water

sprouted from the showerhead. I squeezed soapy water on Erika's back as the suds rolled down to the crack of her ass. It never dawned on me how lucky of a man I was to be with her at that moment. There was no woman alive that could tear me away from her nor give me the urge to cheat. With both hands placed on Erika's shoulders, I slowly turned her around to face me.

"Baby, let me look at you. Don't hide that face from me." I planted kisses on her nose, her eyes, and then those full lips to show her how sincere my words were.

"I love the fuck out of you, Erika Cain! Please don't ever leave me."

Silent for a second, she kissed me back and then spoke the words I needed to hear.

"Tyree, I love you too!"

Wrinkled, the two of us stepped out and wrapped up in bath towels with no intentions of getting dressed. I popped her on the butt as she walked into the bedroom, dropping the towel where she stood. A sign she wanted the dick, I dropped my towel too ready to get inside her sweet spot. On her back with both legs cocked open, that pussy enticed me. Lightly shaved enough to see the lips, my meat got harder the longer I stared at it.

Like a predator, I moved in the direction of the bed slowly towards my late night snack. In a position with both hands, I held on to her hips while my tongue tickled the clitoris before lapping over it back and forth.

It puzzled me how she tasted like strawberries every time I went down on her. Once she released two rounds, it was time to get deep inside her for some good stroking. Long stroking and teasing her, I tried to keep my moans silent as long as possible, but the pleasure made it hard. I held on for a few more minutes before I let go of my bodily fluids. With a scream of satisfaction, she slapped my ass cheeks as I slid off the top of her.

"You do it to me every time, girl! I swear you got a weapon between them legs that will never make me leave your side."

"Yeah, my shit's like sunshine! That is why I can't open my shit to any and everybody. The last thing I need is to kill a nigga." Those words made me glance at her because those were my exact thoughts.

She followed me to the bathroom to wash between her legs while I took a leak. Through the mirror at the double sink, all I could do was stare at the angel while she washed her hands. Naked and stunning, Erika was like a drug that was made only for me because once she dosed me up, my anger disappeared. There was no way I would let another nigga take her from me ever. She's the first person to ever be so close to me, someone I trusted and would kill for again. The bond grew between us that made it hard to leave days at a time for jobs.

In bed with her in my arms, I weighed the options of my profession and relationship. Against my better judgment, I wanted her to travel with me regardless of the potential danger. In my line of business, she was a liability. However, she was an asset. She was a hitta, the Bonnie to my Clyde, Beyoncé to my Jay-Z, Tasha to my Ghost, and any other power couple.

Often, when she slept, I watched those pretty lips and stroked her soft hair. That shit might sound corny as hell, but our heartbeats were in sync when I held her in my arms. It was unthinkable that a killa like me found love in a woman so loyal, caring, and who matched my level of crazy. Pussy whipped, I laid and wondered if I inherited the trait

from that punk ass, sperm donor. Either way, it was cool.
Erika was worth it all.

After laying there for close to an hour, I slipped out to
smoke a blunt and think about life. My life was the best it
had ever been, but something told me this feeling wouldn't
last. Unsure of how shit would unfold with ole boy, I
planned to keep my queen safe by any means necessary. On
the balcony of our condominium, I blew out the smoke
enjoying the buzz that followed behind it.

Back in the bed with a handful of Erika's ass, I dozed off
for a few hours. However, like clockwork, my body woke up
from the visions of those I've killed. Quiet not to disturb
Erika I grabbed some boxers and my phone and went
downstairs.

CHAPTER 1

TYREE LYONS

DEATH REALLY FUCKED my head up mainly since I dropped body after body across the Midwest. Murder for hire kept me paid with a six-figure salary. Over a hundred people lost their lives by my hands, and for that sin, I'm haunted every night. Sometimes the feeling is indescribable, like a vampire with no humanity. I never develop feelings, emotions, or get attach to anyone in my line of work. Sometimes I blamed my dark side on the fucked up genes I inherited and the foster care system.

Every morning when my eyes opened, I knew it was for a reason, yet never understood why. Everything I wanted was in my possession in the material form. My goal in life involved money, survival, and a change in lifestyle. Lord knows I wanted to make a change. However, it wasn't that simple. Taking lives not only kept me paid, but it also helped me pass the time and forget my past.

The bitch that pushed me out of her womb and the sperm donor ass nigga who fucked her disappeared. They left me a bastard and ward of the state. The word family was not something I knew the meaning of nor did I care to.

From age five, a nigga got dealt a bad hand. I got bounced around multiple homes to people who claimed to care about me. The truth is they wanted the check that came with taking me. Two families cared about me, but I ended up fucking things up by fighting too much. As a teenager, the anger build-up caused foster families to reject me as if I wasn't already used to being abandoned.

Being bounced from home to home did some psychological damage to my already fucked up head. Most of the families I got placed with only took me in for the money with no intention to treat me as their own. In front of the social worker, life was great, but when she left, hell resumed. During my stay at the fourth place, two other kids lived there as well. The father Dennis believed in discipline and keeping women in line. He used to beat the shit out of us until enough was enough. One fall night, Dennis came home sauced up on whiskey and grew upset because his dinner wasn't hot enough. The commotion from the kitchen grew so loud that us kids ran to the top of the stairs.

As the oldest, I assured them everything would be okay and to stay on the stairs. At age eleven, I knew a man wasn't supposed to hit a woman, so I crept into the kitchen and grabbed a butcher knife. Without hesitation, I rammed the blade into his gut and twisted it while he stared with bulging eyes. My heartbeat was pounding as I grind my teeth, not feeling an ounce of remorse for my actions. As the blood covered my hand, I took pleasure in watching the piece of shit get a dose of his own medicine. That was my first introduction to taking a life, a memory that will always be embedded in my head.

My foster mother Janet watched horrified and in shock of what had just transpired. Dennis, the bully, fell to the floor holding his stomach. Janet rushed to call 911 and explained to them it was a self-defense situation. The police and ambulance treated her bruises, took a statement, but no charges were filed. I was removed from the home a few days later, but it didn't matter any to me. That was the first time my rage and anger escaped me, leading up to attempted murder. Dennis' bitch ass lived through the ordeal but had to carry a shit bag around for the rest of his life. Forever changed by that event, I never took kindly to a nigga raising a hand to a woman for whatever reason.

Imagine no parents or real family around. Not knowing your background, where you come from. Love and affection were foreign. I didn't know how to give it to anyone or receive it. There were many days I cried and prayed for someone to love me, but later in life, I learned that love doesn't love anybody and adopted the bad boy act. The anger inside had to come out, and one night, I got roped up in some shit with some local thugs. I ended up beating a man to death trying to impress the three teens that were close in age. I never got caught, but it was still murder.

At age eighteen, I was on my own. A counselor connected me to a recruiter of the United States Marines. I decided to give it a shot, so I enlisted. During that period, so many good things happened to me, but a few incidents occurred as well. Being young, smart, and active, the Marine Corp. was a blessing and a curse because I connected with so many men and women that have served before me in Afghanistan and Iraq.

There were times when I wanted to jump on a plane back to Milwaukee, but there was nowhere for me to go. Eventually, they taught me how to grow from a boy to a man, a dangerous man with two hands for weapons. I went from an abandoned young dude to a trained killing machine with brothers and sisters for a lifetime.

One person, in particular, became my ace because our skill set on the shooting range mirrored each other. As a sniper, I needed a spotter, and Tristan became that guy. He was also a sniper with perfect scores. He grew up in Chicago on the south side in dire circumstances. That nigga was just as crazy as me, but his suaveness reminded me of myself.

Our brotherhood grew strong, a bond that meant more than anyone could imagine. He taught me shit that I should've learned from a father. Tristan and I exchanged information when my time was up, and I got discharged from my duties. Once I left the service, the feeling of returning to a city, where no one would be waiting was depressing as fuck. Nevertheless, I sucked it up.

Life as a thirty-two-year-old black man was a struggle, and no one other than another black man would be able to understand. Every day the thought of not making it home due to murder by police surfaced in the minds of every black man who walked the streets. That included me as well, but as a military man, I knew the law and how to handle myself. Although I killed for hire, it didn't define who I was as a person.

⊏⊐

Transitioning back to civilian life wasn't easy. It forced me to stay withdrawn. When I did go out, I dressed in all black, profiled people, and minded my business. Jack Daniels and I became good pals. Phases of emotional depression set in until I receive a random call from a man who was aware of my non-active status. Unknown to me, he never revealed much about himself but knew everything about me. It turned out he was a contractor who wanted to offer me a professional job. Without questions, I accepted, and that is when I knew I had to sober up for what was next to come. I went for the interview a week after the call. It was a blessing because boredom and insanity had almost stroked my nerves.

When I pulled up to the address given, it turned out the interview was like some Charlie Angels type of mess. The man was nowhere in sight. He never showed his face. Instead, the meeting took place over a speaker. Sketchy as it seemed I didn't trip as long as the money was real. He gave details on connections across different cities in every department of government, and knowledge of how I could gain access to more money than I could spend in a lifetime. As a military member, I was privy to confidential information and skills that made me perfect for the job. He explained that I would have to travel to complete his tasks. This included the disposal of bodies and carrying out hit lists. Since I had no name to address the man by, he became "Mr. Anonymous" from that day forward.

The interview turned out to be a four-part training mission that provided the tasks, responsibilities, payment, and tips. Each training session was to get me back in shape, test my skills, and prep me to be the killing machine I was. My hit list consisted of dos and don'ts. High-level officials were off limits. Like previous training, I had to learn to be one with the environment again to study my prey. One thing that was key to it all was to avoid casualties at all cost. Strategy and patience were crucial to learning habits and routines of those who breathed their last breath. After eliminating two bodies without incident, more names came my way from the contractor.

One nigga who had a thirty-thousand-dollar bounty on his head lived a lavish life with rich friends. He partied, and from what I gathered was the man everybody loved to be around. Not knowing much of his history what I did know was his pervert ass had an eye for little girls. Pedophiles didn't deserve to live lavish as he did, a popular white man with money. I stalked him for a week paying close attention to detail until the perfect time to strike. As a night owl, I preferred to attack my prey during the late hours of the night where nothing but darkness and evil shadowed me.

I blended into the crowd but could disappear at any given moment. Dark like midnight, I moved unnoticed, able to adapt to any situation. As a civilian, I was more dangerous than ever with no rules or anyone looking over my shoulder. My life would never be the same, but the common denominator remained, isolation was the only thing I knew. In my line of work, single life was suited for safety purposes. Collateral damage wasn't something I needed on my conscious.

Like on the movies, I kept a safe house in two different locations separate from my permanent home. My gun collection included a McMillan TAC-338A: semi-auto, 7.62 nato rounds, and custom black tip armor piercing rounds, the type that shoot through specific bulletproof glass and armor-plated vehicles. My favorite was the Beretta and .9 mil with a silencer. One night I learned how to make my own ammo for emergencies.

Knives were my second favorite weapon because throwing knives were like throwing darts at a board. My toss was perfect, and in desperate times, I have killed someone quicker in that way. My infatuation with weapons and violence wasn't enough. I earned a brown belt in jiu-jitsu. Hand-to-hand combat was my favorite. It kept us on guards all the time. We never knew who the enemy could be. Bilingual, I learned Spanish and Arabic to serve as a translator. It never hurt to be multi-talented.

Killing for a living was harder than people could imagine sometimes, but I did it the correct way. My military background trained me on how to be a professional killer without leaving a trace. The downside of this life included cold sweats, lack of sleep, and visions of those who died by my hands. Trained not to sleep, I was able to go four days without sleep before my body shut down. Before my solo missions, Tristan used to be my wingman that made things easier. Once separated, I vowed to work alone going forward. I rolled solo because I didn't have any homeboys but also because of what I did. Niggas had big mouths and would get my ass caught up quick from running they trap. Shit, a nigga didn't have a girl either because bitches were quicker to fuck a nigga over. Trust in a woman was something I never had and probably would never experience. Abandoned by the one person who was supposed to have my back was the root cause of my trust issues with women.

I can recall a time in California when a Latino chica flirted with me, but shit never got serious. We were feeling each other for a minute. She was thick as fuck, and her personality kept me interested, but I found out she had a boyfriend. I didn't fuck with other niggas chicks. That brought about drama. I avoided confrontations to spare lives.

CHAPTER 2

ERIKA CAIN

BEFORE IT GOT TOO late at night, I decided to make a quick trip for another three pack of cigarillos. The CITGO had only been a few blocks from home, so I didn't bother to get dressed up. I slid on a pair of leggings, a t-shirt, and a thin hoodie. Either way, my beauty shined. I grabbed my clutch, house keys, and rose gold iPhone 7 then headed out to my Altima. I pushed the start button and scanned for the right song before pulling off. I wondered if all black folks did that shit. By the end of Big Sean's song, I pulled into a parking space in front of my destination.

Once inside I snatched a bag of Flammin' Hot Cheetos, a glazed honey bun, a pack of peanut M&Ms, and a Snickers candy bar. At the register, I asked for a three pack of grape Swishers. As money exchanged between the cashier and my hand, a male voice behind me spoke. I never turned around to see who the guy was until I stepped out of line. When I glanced his way, there stood a caramel goddess who stared back at me. He must have been the sexiest nigga I'd seen in ages. On the low, my ass started to move slowly like a turtle. He had major sex appeal.

"What up, ma?" He leisurely moved towards my direction in an attempt to hold the door open for me.

Who said chivalry was dead? I thought glad to know he had manners.

As he held the door, I couldn't help but notice the deep and prolonged stare down. It was a seductive type of stare down like he wanted to have me for a snack. Right then and there, I felt the pleasure of desire, a flush of warmth between my legs. I remained classy while we continued to check each other out.

"Thanks, not too many men do shit like this without trying to holla."

"I'm not like most men. Maybe we'll see each other again, huh?"

"Maybe." I batted an eye trying to flirt a little bit.

"If we do, you should let me take you out somewhere for a real conversation. Until then, take care and have a good night."

"Thanks. You too."

"Aye, I didn't get your name. I'm Tyree."

"Erika. It's a pleasure to meet you, Tyree," I extended my hand.

Unexpectedly he placed a kiss on the top of it. I damn near lost it when he winked, and then he had the nerve to lick his lips. That had to be the ultimate orgasm winner. It was something about a sexy ass nigga who licked his lips.

With each step towards my ride, I could feel his stare directly on my backside. Once inside my all white Altima with tinted windows, I beeped the horn then pulled off. During the drive, a car followed behind me, and I wondered if it was him. The car turned off after the first set of lights. I had to know more about him because his style of dress was different from what I'm used to.

Dressed GQ smooth, Tyree wore a lightweight black jacket, black collar shirt, and black tie. His swag was impressive. At first glimpse, I thought his ass was a secret service agent or something. Whatever he did for a living I bet he didn't take shit from anyone. He sure left me with something to look forward to if we happened to share the same space again. Single by choice, there wasn't a man who interested me enough to settle down. Tyree appeared to be a possible candidate, but I figured we probably wouldn't see each other again. I kicked back with my snacks for the rest of the night.

Two weeks later around the same time, I ended up bumping into Tyree again. I made a pit stop at CITCO on my way from friend Keisha's house. A smirk crept across my face as I checked him out from head to toe. Again he dressed in all black looking good enough to fuck. I noticed a grape Swisher Sweet packages laid on the counter. I learned he smoked too, a sign we could be smoke buddies.

"Umm, I see you about to get lit," I commented. He turned and flashed a grin, which made my heart flutter.

"You know it. Why you always out at night alone? You should be in the house where it's safe."

"That's where I'm headed but need a three pack of Vegas," I shot back.

I found it refreshing that he showed concern for my well-being. In a good mood, all I could do was smile as our eyes locked in a gaze. The dimples made me want to melt, but when he licked those lips, my knees got weak for a millisecond.

"You must be zooted already," Tyree asked.

"I'm straight. It's just funny that the last time we saw each other, you were the one making a comment," I reminded him.

Dressed in a pair of denim jeans, a cute dressy black top, and a light jacket, I looked sexy as hell, glad he was able to see the dressed side of me. Harmless flirting between the two of us made seeing each other worth wild. Like deja vu, he escorted me to my car again, giving me another chance to examine his handsome face. Once I got inside, he closed my door and wished me a good night.

Almost immediately after I drove away, I couldn't help but notice in the rearview mirror, his vehicle had literally caught up behind me. My first thought was that he was a cute psycho about to follow me. Before I had a chance to panic, he made a left turn at the streetlights while I kept straight. I let out a sigh of relief as I made it back to the crib. Of course, I hit my girl line to let her know I made it safe.

"Hey Siri, call Keisha," I instructed. As I undressed out of my clothes, the phone kept ringing, but I knew she wasn't asleep that fast. All of a sudden, she answered.

"What up, E?"

"What took you so long, bitch? I thought you went to sleep that fast. Guess what? I just saw that dude again. His name is Tyree." I snatched the phone and walked over to grab a nightgown from the drawer to slip on.

"On what, you take a picture?"

"Girl naw, what I was supposed to say, smile for the camera my friend wants to see you," I said sarcastically. "Trust my word, he's fine. I'll try to get a picture if we meet again. Anyway, I called to let you know I made it safe. I'm about to lie back until I fall asleep. I have a busy morning at the Center. We partnered with a few businesses to do a clothing drive, so I expect more than ten bags of assorted items, not to mention its mock interview sessions." I let out a deep sigh just thinking about it.

"Have fun with that! I'll chat with you tomorrow, girl," Keisha stated.

"Peace out."

The call automatically disconnected as I laid my phone on the nightstand. I snuggled up comfortably in bed with no plan to get up again. In search of the remote, I just used my voice command device, Cortana, to turn on *The Golden Girls*. That show always put me to sleep. It never failed. I always passed out by the third show.

⊏▭⊐

My name is Erika Cain. Behind the smiles, laughs, and persona, I was a depressed person who found comfort in smoking marijuana and watching Netflix. The death of my mom took a toll on my mental state to the point that all I did was hibernate in my condominium. It was easy to put on a front and not display the real me to the everyday world. Those I met admired my bubbly attitude and loving personality, but if they only knew. I was wearing a mask, concealing the pain, addiction, and loneliness. Although depression consumed me, I never thought about suicide or anything to that extent. Instead, I rolled a blunt, grabbed a laptop, and put my feelings into writing.

It wasn't until three months later that I found a purpose and a way to give back. I turned my sadness into something positive that could assist those down on their luck. With the inheritance money, I decided to meet with the lawyer for direction in ownership of a building. From there, I searched for a building to lease and set up a nonprofit organization to help women and children in need. Giving back to the community was important to me because not only it was the right thing to do, but also one has to give to receive. Blessed was the only way to describe my life. Therefore, I spread my blessings to others. I called the place Leap of Faith Center.

I helped women and men complete job applications and provided transportation to their interviews. There was a location in the building for tutoring the neighborhood kids as well. Lastly, a crew served food on the weekends. Too often, some kids only ate during the week at school. No child should ever go hungry, and I made it my duty to feed as many kids as possible. Doing for others took my mind off my troubles.

As the owner of the establishment, I hired ten staff members, five men and five women who made sure things operated properly. Two of the women, Ms. Pam and Ms. Susan, had previous experience in running an organization. They also served as the elders and kept everyone in line yet gave love those they assisted. Within the first month of working together, I was glad I'd chosen those ten to assist me.

Three times a week, I made an appearance to check on everything, do paperwork, and miscellaneous tasks. Proud of my accomplishment, it felt delightful doing good to make up for the bad shit I did. On select Saturday afternoons, I helped serve lunch as a way to network with the boys and girls. I did a good deed to help right my wrongs.

Close to a year since my mom passed, I got up on Saturday mornings to grab a coffee and some flowers and drove by to Graceland Cemetery. When I arrived, my typical routine was to change her flowers, dust off her headstone, and sit. The serenity of the place helped calm my anxiety as I had a conversation about the recent events in my life. I went so far to pull up the few videos saved on my phone just to hear her voice and laugh. Time at the cemetery kept me from snapping out at folks but more so made me appreciate life itself.

Losing a parent was the worst feeling I'd ever had to experience. The emptiness and dialing her number to get no answer were overwhelming at times, not to mention holidays weren't the same. What ate me up the most inside was Mother's Day, and seeing moms out with their kids. Tears fill my eyes no matter how hard I tried to hold back. Not knowing my father was tough enough, but to lose my best friend was devastating. Truly my best friend, my mom knew me better than I knew myself. With so much life to live, lung cancer took it three months before she turned fifty years old. Crushed, I shut down. I realized how Kanye West felt when his mom died. I felt his pain and understood how life-altering a situation like that took on a person.

I always got a little depressed after my visits, so to cope, I rolled up a fat blunt and watched her favorite black and white movie *What Ever Happened to Betty Jane* starring Betty Davis. With no real social life, I stayed home most of the time unless Keisha got me out to party. Even though I was a cocky bitch, I remained humbled. Confidence made me feel like I was the most beautiful woman on earth. A redbone chick, my skin was flawlessly smooth with the perfect bone structure. A mixture of my father's white gene and my mother's black gene, my body was evidence of the black side with curves of my Apple Bottom ass. I had a head full of naturally curly hair that I kept straightened.

Almost five feet eight inches tall, my looks alone got me almost anything I desired. Yes, I'm one of those females who believed looks were everything, but my street game backed me up. Independent, I did for myself, but the offers from men in the form of men or cars, I accepted. I'm the daughter of a pimp and madam. Yeah you read that right, a pimp and madam for parents isn't something I like to brag about, but such is life.

Growing up, my mom schooled me on the game by age ten. She always told me not to depend on a man for anything. While little girls played with dolls and jumped rope, my mom taught me how to slit men pockets for their wallets. She also taught me how to use Visine in a man's drink. It knocked him out long enough to hit a lick and disappear. The skills I acquired from her were survival tactics in a dominant male world. Once I started dating, any guy I took home was put to the test by my mom. It was as if she was a human lie detector or part psychic because she could shake their hand, then tell me about him.

Her number one rule was never get attached to a man, no matter what he said or did. It wasn't clear to me what she meant until I got old enough to see how full of shit men were. Men said anything to get sex then disappeared like a deadbeat dad. When it came to parenting, she disciplined me as needed. Nonetheless, her love for me was unconditional. Eventually, when I grew into adulthood, she didn't encourage me to adopt her way of life. Instead, she made sure I went to college and invested my money in something that I could be proud of. Each woman in our family possessed both street and book smarts in conjunction with being smooth criminals. Patrice Cain was one of a kind woman. In life, a mother is the one person in the world that a daughter confided in, she was my confidant.

In the end, I took my path and didn't become a madam. However, I did use men for my own personal gain. Men were nothing but a tool to be used. With no regard, I treated them how they treated women, like a piece of meat. The animosity inside of me towards men stemmed from the lack of a male role model. I vowed to follow my mom's rules and never fall in love with a man. Love was a dangerous thing that got many people fucked up, fucked over, or killed. Therefore, I refused to fall into any of those categories.

CHAPTER 3

TYREE LYONS

I STOOD in line behind this exotic redbone at the counter paying for a bunch of junk food. It didn't take me long to notice the three-pack of Cigarillos that she had too. Usually, I found women who smoked unattractive, but I caught a side profile of her sun-kissed skin that exposed her perfect bone structure. Baby girl possessed a natural beauty. She didn't have to dress half-naked or wear makeup. She was that gorgeous.

"Damn, you about to get twisted," I said before I knew it.

She never turned around to peer back at me as the clerk put her items in a white plastic bag. The cashier rang my stuff, not wasting time as he continued to stare me down. I tossed a twenty on the counter, retrieved my change and roll-ups.

I noticed shorty had prolonged her exit as she lingered by the door with a raised brow. She smirked as I put the Swisher package in my inside jacket pocket. All I could do was eyeball her in awe. Shit, I wanted to get her pregnant. I held the door for her as we walked out together and continued our chat.

She seemed like someone I could call a friend if nothing more, but I definitely wanted to smash. In my line of work, living the single life was best for survival, but I was willing to change for her. We continued small chat outside before we exchanged names. I watched her get inside the Altima and drive away as her plates became registered in my head. I got in my ride and drove behind her hoping that she didn't think I was following her. It just happened to be the same direction to my place, but I turned off. Headed home for a little rest, my life traveling required R&R whenever possible.

Within a forty-eight hour time span, I was on the road to Chi-town to cancel some dude who went by the name Lil Foot on the street. Apparently, his ass had a birth deformity that resulted in his left foot being smaller than the other. In my opinion, with that name, he should've been a humbled man. Instead, he hit women and didn't know how to keep his mouth closed. That shit was crazy as hell to me. Real men are never supposed to put hands on a woman unless it's consensual. The client had specific instructions— Lil Foot's death had to be nice and slow. Those types of jobs satisfied my thirst to kill low-life niggas who deserved it. Abuse of any kind towards a woman was punishable by death.

On the way there, I couldn't help but think about shorty from the gas station. I didn't believe in coincidence at all. However, it was destiny or something that kept bringing us together. Every time we came in contact, it was for blunt wraps or snacks, a good sign that she was a low-key type of chick. It was more to meet the eye with her, and I planned to find out more when I returned to Milwaukee.

Focused on my task, I pulled into the Hyde Park area,

ready to check in at the Hyatt Place Chicago. Close to six in the morning, the sun still hadn't risen making time seem earlier than what it was. Strolling right through the doors, I left my car with the valet as I approached the sista at the desk.

"Good morning sir, welcome to the Hyatt Place Chicago. How may I assist you?" she greeted.

"Hi. Do you have anything available for two or three nights? Any room is fine with me as long as it's clean. No offense."

"None taken, sir," the young lady shot back as she kept her eyes on the computer screen. "There are three doubles and several king rooms located on various floors? Any preferences?"

"No, I'll take a king for three nights," I answered as I pulled my wallet from my pocket.

"Umm, you are aware check-in isn't until later, right?" she questioned.

I slide six Benjamin Franklin's on the counter and grinned knowing that my charm would get her to make an exception. Her eyeballs widened at the president as she giggled.

"Well, we can make a special exception since there are a few rooms vacant. However, to keep from getting in trouble, I'll need a credit or debit card for incidentals."

I agreed and compiled by giving her a debit card and waited while she took my information and provided the key. I headed for my room, avoiding all cameras. With only a medium sized duffle bag, I stepped into the elevator with an older white couple. Almost instantly, they stared me down until I unzipped my jacket exposing my dog tags. Their postures loosened as the woman flashed a fake ass smile. When we hit the seventh floor, and the doors opened, they stepped off and had the nerve to face me.

"Thanks for your service, young man," the older man said as the doors slowly closed. I shook my head in disgust and couldn't help but to think white folks were a muthafucking trip, but that's the Amerikkka we live in.

Up to the ninth floor, I stepped off the elevator to pure silence. I walked down the hall to room 917 and entered it. Before getting comfortable, I checked the room for anything out of the norm then tossed my bag on the bed. In deep thought of how to torture and dispose of Lil Foot's body, nobody knew Chicago better than my Marine brother Tristan, so I hit him up.

"Oorah!" I yelled into the phone.

He did the same thing before I wasted no time explaining my reason for calling. In so many words, I filled him in on my new freelance work and the task I had to complete. Not sure where I'd catch my target, I needed a few options as far as abandoned spots to take him. Off top Tristan told me of two places that I saved in my memory bank, I never wrote shit down that could incriminate myself. Before we disconnected, he encouraged me to join him for a drink afterward to clear my mind. Of course, I agreed.

A half hour later, I'd changed clothes and headed for breakfast. The Original Pancake House was located five minutes away from my hotel and target. With a picture of dat nigga's ugly mug, it was a matter of time before I caught him. Just as I finished my food, the burner phone went off with word ole boy was driving his girl's maroon Passat. Intel led me down S Cottage Grove Avenue and to a twelve-story brick apartment building on my left. Sure enough, the Passat sat in front of the building, but I didn't park. Instead,

I circled the block once more to do surveillance before I doubled back to place a tracker under the car.

One of the abandoned spots my broski told me about wasn't far away either. I retreated to the hotel in order to get a plan together. I managed to get a quick nap and something to eat before the all-night stakeout. People were predictable in their everyday habits, and he was no different. It was only a matter of time until he let his guard down.

The tracker led me to Golden Fish and Chicken, which was close to that apartment from earlier. I figured his bitch made him grab food before he hit the streets for the night. I nodded my head as I could visually see my plan unfold. Before he could spot me, I pulled off and headed south on S Cottage Grove Avenue, parked, and hit my lights.

Parked behind a two-door Honda Accord Coupe, I was in position and ready to snatch that little foot nigga. I watched the little Kat Williams lookalike pull up, kill the engine, and hop out with a big ass bag and a soft drink in hand. When he entered the building, I swiftly exited my ride, gun on my hip, in murder mode. To keep from looking suspect, I retrieved the Black & Mild from my pocket and lit it. Pacing the pavement blowing smoke, my spidey senses alerted me to get in position. A slight squeak sound caused me to look in the direction of the door to witness him coming down the steps. I quickly brushed past him on the sidewalk too close for comfort and stuck my gun in his back.

"If you make a sound yo' ass is dead? Do you understand?" I demanded through gritted teeth as I bounded both of his hands.

"Maaaan!" he responded.

"Yo, what the fuck did I say? Move ya ass to my ride." Without a fight, he slid in the backseat with his hands zip-tied behind his back.

I drove a short distance to the back of the brick building where Tristan sent me. Lil Foot remained quiet when I snatched him and my bag from the car. Upon entering, I held him at gunpoint as we moved inside. I held my phone in the other hand as its flashlight guided us. Using my five senses while maneuvering, I found the light switch, scanned the empty space, and then spotted a wooden chair, dusty circle table, and a bunch of other cluttered shit. At that moment he knew shit was a wrap for him.

"Take a seat nigga. Yo' ass better not try shit either," I hissed.

Careful not to leave any traces of myself, I retrieved a pair of latex gloves, and then I removed a few necessities from my black bag. I freed his hands of the zip ties, but quickly tied them back up behind his back. I tied his feet as well making sure the knots were double secured.

"Nigga, who the fuck are you, a black John Wick or some shit?"

"I'm glad to see you got jokes. It's a shame that'll be your last one!" I spat as I moved towards him with a box cutter and spray bottle filled with lemon juice. That nigga's eyes bugged out like a cartoon character.

Lil Foot bodied started to tremble. His body wasn't equipped for the torture I inflicted upon him. Without showing a drop of mercy, I went ahead and took him out of his misery, sending him to his maker with a quick snap of the neck. I put a pillowcase over his head then quickly grabbed my shit hitting the lights on my way out. The murder rate in the city was already high, but that nigga had just been added to the count. In a smooth move, I disappeared from the scene without being seen.

I stopped at Subway after the job to change clothes and shoes. After I ordered two six inch Italian ham and turkey subs, I gave a sandwich and my old kicks to a random homeless guy who sat outside the restaurant. Afterward, I joined Tristan for a few drinks at The Violet Hour. In his typical style, he tried to hook me up when I entered, but my lack of interest for the weave wearing chick caused her to catch an attitude. She couldn't handle my bluntness, something most women couldn't.

"Bro, you said join you for a drink, not some random hood rat," I retorted. In no mood to deal with strangers, I instructed the bartender to keep the shots of Bombay coming as I adjusted to the atmosphere.

"My bad bro, I thought a chick would loosen you up. Let's move around to the other end of the bar," he suggested. "Pussy always makes a nigga feel better after a job," he added.

"Not me," I shot back. "Nowadays making a woman happy was a full-time job. A nigga ain't got time for attitudes and shit."

That was a prime reason I didn't like to date, living the bachelor life wasn't too bad since I was always on the road. Focused on killing, sex wasn't a necessity, but my needs were met whenever.

We took a few steps over to the other side of the bar in a better position to view the entrance and exits.

I took a seat on the stool and tossed back the double shot of liquor. "Ahh!" The burn caught me on the way down causing me to burp quietly.

"What the hell you been doing with yourself?" Tristan questioned in between sips of his Hennessy.

"Nigga, where you want me to start," I joked as we drank and reminisced for several hours.

CHAPTER 4

ERIKA CAIN

SEVERAL WEEKS WENT by before Tyree showed his face again. I had begun to wonder about him. Never a thirsty type of woman, he definitely had me feeling some type of way. While inside, Larry strolled through the aisle, and out of instinct, I turned up my nose in disgust at the sight of him. That nigga was salty that his sister got rocked by me for talking about my deceased mother. Unbothered by Larry's presence, Tyree's defensive stance proved he had my back in case shit escalated. That small gesture meant the world to me. Larry was weak like his sister. I dared him to utter a word in my direction. Once he didn't, I continued on with my business.

Afterward, Tyree and I conversed in between moving outside of the gas station, similar to the last time. When he suggested we go smoke together, it took a minute for me to decide. Not knowing if I should go or not, I took a chance since it was daylight. He had me follow behind him to a safe house two blocks around the corner from the CITGO. Once I realized exactly where his house was located, my safety antennas calmed down. I was in close proximity to my condo.

I parked and climbed out of my Altima only to get inside of his vehicle. Within fifteen minutes, we sat chilling as if we had known each other since grade school. He had a mix of music playing low in the background. Although he didn't offer much personal information about himself, the chemistry was undeniable. Neither of us talked much at first, but the body language said it all. It surprised the entire time me how random it was that I was chilling with a stranger.

During our session, my inquisitiveness got the best of me as my eyes constantly searched for items that would help me learn more about him. How a person kept their car gave away things about them. In his case, everything was so clean, and there wasn't anything out of place. Unable to remain silent any longer, I broke the silence with a little small talk.

"If you don't mind me asking, tell me something about you I should know." At first, he looked as if I asked for his social security number but eventually spoke up.

"I served in the military for a few years, and because of that, I stay to myself. I try to mind my business and be on that lay low type of shit. Feel me?"

"Yes. I stay to myself too. Besides hanging with my girl Keisha, I smoke, run my organization, and chill."

"Sounds like my type of chick!"

"Maybe I am, maybe I'm not. Either way, I'm enjoying this random ass session.

Ha, "Why you say it like that? Don't act like you not semi-feeling a nigga. Shit, I'm feeling you. You probably think I'm a stalker ass nigga, but the truth is we were meant to meet."

"Is that so?" I tried hard not to blush or show interest, but I knew better.

"Yeah, you can't act like you don't feel the same way. I can read people ma, and every time you look at me, those eyes let me know."

"Let you know what exactly?"

"That you digging a nigga just like I'm digging you. On some real shit, I usually don't do stuff like this at all. I'm a reserved type of man, solo, and low key. Something about you got me taking a risk."

"I haven't known you long enough, but I won't lie. You caught my attention. You seem like a cool dude though. I could see us as smoke buddies."

"Only time will tell, right? Until then, I gotta take care of some business. It's been cool chopping it up after so many run-ins. Be safe."

"Yeah, I agree to chill with you turned out pretty sway," I commented while gesturing to get out.

"I'll hit you up but please don't get pissed if it's at odd hours."

"Oh, I put my phone on Do Not Disturb through the night anyway. Be cool."

"Smart. See you around gorgeous."

We had to go our separate ways, but I knew it wouldn't be the last time. In fact, it had been the first time I had been in the company of a man in a long time. I liked the way he made me feel within a short period of time. I closed the passenger door and strutted while he watched me walked away.

Not in the car long enough to turn on the music, I made it home ready to tear up some food. First, I slipped out of my shoes, put my stuff down on the counter, and scanned through the fridge. My taste buds craved leftover steak and potatoes, so I heated it up in the Black & Decker convection oven. While waiting, my movement around the kitchen from the cabinet to fridge turned into dance moves. When the timer went off, I retrieved the nice, juicy piece of meat as it still sizzled. I drizzled A-1 steak sauce across it sure to saturate every inch. At the counter, I stared at the plate fit for a stoner that screamed "eat me" so I sat in dead silence and enjoyed every bit of my meal.

Full and fresh from a warm shower, Tyree kept popping in my head, causing me to laugh out loud. I checked the time eager to call Keisha ready to spill the beans about the black James Bond. To kill time until nine, I twisted a Swisher and turned on *She's Gotta Have It* on Netflix. I recalled the man who caught my eye, not able to control the wild thoughts. Halfway through episode four, the phone rang.

"What up, chick? I made it home."

"I was waiting for a text. Girl, guess what? I ran into Tyree at the gas station again. My silly ass had a smoke session with him and everything. He is cool as hell."

"What? Not in your condo I hope," Keisha sounded concerned.

"Hell naw, we chilled in his car not far from my place. I'm not that crazy, although he got potential," I joked then took two more puffs before butting the cigar.

"Do you sista but be careful. Aye, we need to go shopping soon so scan your calendar. I'm about to shower and eat and take my ass to sleep. I'll hit you up."

"Alright. I'm about to turn in myself. I have a lot to do at the Center."

"Night."

"Night."

For the rest of the week, I poured myself into the Center as I completed the inventory and worked with a few young girls. Two of the three were on the right track with goals to get their degree and mature as young adults. It gave me comfort to know my words and actions were positively being used. Although I smoked damn near every day, it never affected my behavior or duties while at the Center. If anything, I found myself providing the emotional support and empathy others failed to give those who sought help.

All of my good deeds for the week drained me, but things got sweet when Tyree texted me. He was out of town, so we couldn't see each other, but the phone was the next best thing. Talking on the phone had never been my cup of tea, but I'd text all day long. I had saved his number under *Fuck-Me-Eyes* because that's exactly how I felt whenever in his presence. The more we chatted, the more I looked forward to chilling with him again. In some kind of fantasy, I had sex dreams several nights in a row after talking to him. The dude had me head over heels.

CHAPTER 5

TYREE LYONS

I GREW CONVINCED the third time had been the charm meeting up with Erika at the same spot. A nigga wasn't complaining though. I honestly looked forward to it because shorty was right. I noticed the wrinkles in her forehead had creased, and I wondered why. Some big sloppy looking nigga walked inside, and it was evident she had beef or disliked him.

"Aye, you good, ma? Do I need to fuck that nigga up for you?"

"Naw I'm good. I fucked his sister up a few months back. She disrespected my mama."

"On what? Let me find out you a street fighter," I joked. My comment made her crack a smile. Light bright was the first name that popped into my head, so that became her new nickname.

"I'm not a fighter but will fuck someone up for disrespecting my mom or me."

"Shit, if you ain't scared we can go a block a two from here and smoke in my car. I got a safe house for emergencies and shit. It's a low-key spot where you can park your car.

Trust me. All I wanna do is get to you know, no touching or bullshit, promise."

"Nigga, you could be a friendly psycho for all I know. I must admit you are fine as fuck. The most we can do is hit a blunt together, but I gotta roll that bitch," she demanded. She flashed a smile then proceeded towards the exit.

"Dude, you funny as hell. I like you already because you talk hella shit, ma."

I followed behind her all while taking a mental picture of the dude in my head. If she gave me the word, his punk ass was dead just like that. We walked towards her car as my steps delayed so that I could watch her strut. Erika had a snatched body with a mean walk. Without getting caught staring, she climbed inside her Altima eyeing me wearing a mischievous grin. All I could do was drop my head and laugh because she was too damn cute.

A woman who joked and could make me laugh had some potential to get in my circle, which was small like a period. Erika followed closely behind me all while I was about to break one of my rules— exposing one of my locations. Through two sets of streetlights and a right turn down an alley, I whipped my shit and shut off the engine. The tinted window Altima backed in beside me.

When she opened the passenger door and got inside, I sat with a laser-focused gaze on her. There had been a sack and blunt ready for her. From the looks of things, she seemed comfortable while rolled up and sparked. She blushed, and it made her even more attractive to me. Once we got past the awkwardness and the weed got in our system, we sat and chilled like homies from around the way.

I knew she was worth the time of day when our paths crossed at the same place. It was beyond a sexual attraction that made me interested in her. The way she talked turned me on too. There was a certain spice in her tone, switch in her walk, and a chill personality. Women could change up at any time. Therefore, I played my cards smart. I had to learn her likes dislikes, triggers, and other traits.

With the exchange of numbers, we chatted on several occasions while I moved around from city to city. Erika captured the inner me who craved attention but couldn't express that need. Too soon to know if shit would move beyond smoking buddies, I fucked with her. Shit, I couldn't wait to fuck her either, but I knew that would happen down the line.

In my profession, I kept contact with others to a minimal until Erika came into the picture. Although there was a difference between being lonely and alone, I was glad to have met Erika. We chatted on the phone, but we gave each other distance careful not to be overbearing. In case shit didn't work out, I wanted our lives to remain less complicated as possible. Not sure what the hell women wanted, didn't want, liked, or otherwise, I took notes from Erika. Oblivious to a lot of shit when it came to women, it grew easy to avoid they ass which I'd did a good job at doing.

I found myself thinking about Erika more than I should've, but shit happened for a reason. She had me feeling some type of way. Better yet, she had become an occupant in my head. In doing so, it made me reflect on my encounters with other women. While in the military, I had encountered all types of women, aggressive ass women too.

One time on a stakeout, I recalled a time when I served with this chick whose parents were from Iran. She grew up in America from age ten through adulthood. One night on

24-hour duty, she tried to come on to me, and I'm talking aggressively. She was far from shy and knew what she wanted. I remember she threw me for a loop when she tried to pry into my personal business. The conversation went something like this.

"You are too handsome not to have a girlfriend. Why is that?"

"I had a fucked up childhood. Besides, women can't be trusted. No offense."

"None was taken. And for the record, not all women are the same." She winked and slightly tilted her head to the left.

"Maybe not, but that's how I feel."

"So what about me?" She stood with her arms folded.

"What about you?" Slightly confused by all the questions, I answered them anyway.

"Am I your type? Better yet, would you fuck me?" she bluntly asked.

"Damn girl, you a wild one. To answer your question, No, I'm good, and I mean that in a nice way."

"Oh, so you too good for Iranian pussy?" she spat.

All I could do was laugh that shit off because ole girl was nuts, and I didn't want any parts of that shit. Thankfully we were interrupted by another Marine who came to relieve me of duty. I'm glad I dodged that bullet. I had a feeling that she was the type of chick I would've had to kill.

The bright headlights flashed in my face, which brought me back to reality as my target prepared to pull off in the night. Carefully, I followed from a distance determined to take him out before sunrise. From prior experience, sometimes plans fell through causing a backup option. To avoid witnesses, I patiently waited for the perfect moment. In the meantime, patience and a visual of Erika kept me sane long enough to wait out the crowds of folks who departed the party. The once large crowd dispersed into a few folks lingering around. I took the cue and exited my vehicle in creep mode, not skipping a beat. By the time I snuck up on my prey, it had been too late for him to react.

Back at the hotel, I showered right away to get the stench of death off of me. Each time I played the reaper, I lost something in return. Another job completed earned me more cash than some folks made in a lifetime. After a job, I could never go to sleep. Instead, it left me up like a zombie. I lay in bed with a hand placed behind my head and the other placed on my chest. A dead silence had filled the room as my mind worked on overdrive, mainly Erika filled the space. There were so many unknowns involved with getting close to her, all of my own accord, of course. I didn't know shit about how to make a woman happy or how to keep my killer instincts intact.

Ready to see E, I had one more job before I could pack up and hit the road. That damn girl had my nose open from just a few moments together. For the simple fact that her presence alone kept my interest meant she had broken down a barrier that no one else could ever do. Erika was a beautiful, intelligent, and captivating woman. I needed her to mine.

CHAPTER 6

ERIKA CAIN

ENJOYING A LAZY, warm Saturday afternoon, I lay out in my bed as I enjoyed the cool breeze from the black oscillating floor fan. Not ready to get up yet, I snacked on a bag of cool ranch Doritos and tuned into *Being Mary Jane*. It wasn't until after two o'clock when I climbed out the bed. My girl Keisha hit my line about the All White Affair, so of course, we had to go stunt.

Fresh from a warm shower, I felt so good my body swayed to the music as I two-stepped all the way to the closet. I needed something that screamed, "I'm sexy and not desperate" so I used my hand to scan through the selection of clothing items until my eyes noticed the white sleeveless dress.

"Yes!" I shouted.

I held it in front of me then quickly slide it on, careful not to get it dirty with makeup. Wearing white wasn't something I did a lot of, but I kept a few items for occasions like the All White Affair. If you ever saw the movie *White Chicks* with Shawn and Marlon Wayans, you would understand how anticipated the event was each year. The only thing different was we weren't in the damn Hamptons.

In front of the body length mirror, the knee-length dress fit perfect as I modeled it. The see-through slit ran from the inside of the right shoulder down to the side of my stomach. It showed just enough cleavage without exposing the twins up top. In the back, the small of my back was opened. It was exposed right along with the tip of my tattoo. The downside to the outfit was that a bitch had to wear a thong, but I toughed it out.

Naturally beautiful, I applied a nice coat of "Kinda Sexy" MAC lipstick then rubbed my lips together. I flashed a smile to make sure nothing was on my pearly whites. I smelled like Dolce & Gabbana Light Blue. That was my favorite perfume hands down.

Keisha called within a matter of minutes. I didn't want to hear her mouth about me not being ready. Her ass always claimed that it took me too long to prep. I told her it takes time when you aim for perfection. She didn't know anything about that. Don't get me wrong. That's my girl, but she had a way of throwing shade when something didn't work out in her favor. Nevertheless, she was about her money, plus she had a bad habit of cussing a bum nigga out. We shared those two similarities.

Keisha and I met one night five years ago in the most awkward situation that resulted in a friendship. At a kick-back on the Southside with a so-called friend, named Raquel, I learned a true lesson about the word friend. Out of jealousy, I was almost a victim in a fucking brawl set up by Raquel, but Keisha kept the peace and interjected. Keisha was also friends of Raquel's however, after that shady shit, we both kept our distance from her. The two of us met up over drinks and food a few times, and a bond slowly followed.

I made myself a promise before leaving the house, to not swindle or take anybody's man or wallet. The night was all about dancing, drinking, and creating memories. I knew it wouldn't be anyone who would catch my eye or match my fly. When I made it outside, Keisha was parked in my driveway, checking herself in the visor mirror.

"Damn bitch, you fine as hell!" Keisha yelled.

"Thanks, girl! It's just a little something. You know what Kat Williams said, I gotta get my hater game up, and summer is almost over," I joked.

Gucci Mane bumped from her Lincoln Navigator truck. I put my arms in the air and did a two-step. Trap music always made me groove.

"You a fool, girl!"

"But you know I'm right," I added opening the driver's door to my 2016 Lexus, white on the outside peanut butter on the inside. It was a birthday gift from an old fling that shall remain nameless. I didn't drive it that much because I loved my Altima like a baby.

Inside I laid my clutch in the passenger seat, closed my door, and started the engine. I fastened my seatbelt, pushed the play button on the CD player, then slide on my Chanel sunglasses. Beyoncé and Nicki Minaj glared through the speakers. Keisha looked at me as we nodded our heads. She drove off as I followed behind her.

Still daylight, I cruised through the streets as if I owned them, bobbing my head to the music. When we hit the expressway, I turned up the volume when Dreezy and Gucci Mane came on. Ratchet music got me so crunk sometimes that it was hard to remain ladylike. Keisha turned on her left blinker to switch lanes. Our exit was nearby as I followed behind. My hair lightly blew in the wind as both windows were halfway down. Traffic came to a halt when we hit a right onto Wells Street. Everybody and they mama tried to get a decent parking spot at the Wisconsin Center.

You would have thought that I was a celebrity the way people stared at me pulling up. With the touch of a button, the top lifted until it closed me in. All eyes were on me when I stepped out the sports car. I loved the attention more from the women than men, only because I had them bitches scared that I would cuff any man in sight. Like a boss, Keisha and I strutted with confidence ready to have fun.

The closer we got to the door, two men, in particular, stood out to me. One of them was at least six foot five, and the other was barely six feet. With my shades on, I eyed the sexy bearded chocolate man. He was like a candy bar that I wanted to nibble on. In the line, along with groups of people, I slide my rose gold iPhone from my clutch.

"Aye girl, did I tell you TeTe got suspended again?" Keisha started small talk as the line slowly moved forward.

"What? Your little sister is bad as hell girl. Why does she be acting up all the time?"

"I don't know. Talking to her is a waste of time and breath. My mama said she plans to ship her ass to her daddy."

"That might help. I hope that it does. This is a cold world, and TeTe is not ready. I'm glad my mama put me on the game before she passed away."

Our place in line advanced further to the door of admissions. I retrieved my ticket from the zip part of my clutch.

"Wow, are you a part of the show tonight, young lady?"

My face slightly frowned as my brows wrinkled. I was in no mood for the corny pickup lines. I turned around with a fake smile only to find the same bearded man from outside. Speechless at first, I managed to speak.

"Oh no, I'm not. I'm just here to enjoy the affair. Thanks for the compliment though." He wore a grin as if it was a high school prom and he wanted to ask for a dance.

"I usually don't approach a female in this manner, like a thirsty nigga, but you are so damn fine. You are hands down the best looking woman in here. I'm not just talking shit either. Little mama, you bad, and I would love to know you better."

With Keisha in my eyesight, I contemplated whether or not to entertain or diss him. Against my better judgment, I indulged. Keisha had some person's ear, and it didn't look like she'd miss me. Like a gentleman, he escorted me to the bar as if we came together as a date. The entire time he remained by my side as if he was my personal bodyguard.

"I didn't get your name," I said while we waited for a bartender to assist us.

"I'm Bishop. And yours?"

"Erika," I replied without batting an eye.

He was not the type of man who typically caught my attention. Finally, a tall, slender white guy leaned in to ask what we wanted.

"I'll have a Jack Coke, please," I ordered.

"Give me a Jack on the rocks," Bishop voiced as his sexy voice made me quiver.

Aware of my surroundings, I scanned the room then quickly watched the bartender finish making my drink.

Before I could toss a twenty on the counter, he whispered to me, "Don't insult me, beautiful. I got your drink, and however more you want," he insisted. The entire time he never lost his prolonged eye contact. He also kept biting his lip. That gesture had been my weakness with sexy ass men.

"Thanks, I appreciate it, but one is all I need. You see the car I drove. I can't mess up my baby girl," I joked in an effort to change topics.

"Hell yeah, I saw you pull up looking like a boss chick in that Lexis. You got to taste and class, something many women lack nowadays. Plus, you like the same type of whiskey as me."

Without blushing as much as I wanted to, I held my composure and took a sip of my drink before speaking. We moved into a corner for a little more privacy to hear each other better. People stood everywhere with cocktails in hand until the event officially started.

"Ha, thank you! I was taught to act like a lady at all times. You never know who I might meet."

Before the night ended, we swapped numbers to keep in touch. Given that Tyree and I weren't official, I believed in having options. Men came a dime a dozen. Although it was clear, Tyree was the man who interested me the most. Bishop was a big sexy nigga, and the type I wanted to give a shot.

━━

The next day I stayed in bed and watched *The Golden Girls* from seven until three in the afternoon. Lazy Sundays were the best because all I did was ate, smoked, and slept. I lived simple and chilled, which was fine with me. Growing up as the only child I learned no company was better than having folks around me who only wanted to use me. Besides, as a homebody with food and smoke, life was good.

Later that night, Tyree hit my line, which had become a

routine for us. I got excited every time. I was without a doubt digging him. Careful not to let him know my true feelings, I continued to play the field and kept my options open. Time moved on, and it hadn't been my intention to toy with the hearts of two men, but it happened anyway. Each man was different and an adventure of some kind that kept me entertained. Imagine being given a choice to test drive two of your favorite cars— a Lamborghini and a Corvette.

By the time Monday morning came around, I woke up seconds before the alarm refreshed. At a leisurely pace, I climbed out of bed, placing both feet on the floor as I remained seated. Two yawns later I'd gotten all the way up turning on the radio for motivation to get ready. I shuffled towards the bathroom to pee then stripped for a shower. While washing myself, the mere thought of Tyree entered my head. I rinsed clean using the detachable showerhead, giving my woo-ha extra attention. The warm, hard thrusting water trickled upon my lower lips, causing a ticklish sensation. Afterward, I proceeded with my routine for the day.

In such a joyful mood, I made a stop at Dunkin' Donuts for two dozen assorted pastry sweets. The first to arrive at the Leap of Faith Center, I turned on lights, booted up computers, and made coffee. I used a napkin to grab a frosted chocolate donut with sprinkles then headed to my desk. Not waiting to sit down, I took two bites, savoring the sweet dough. I hoped to get a sugar rush to help push through the paperwork that waited for my attention. There had been invoices along with other bills that needed to be paid.

"Good morning!" a voice called out from the main space of the office.

I took a few more bites before rising from my seat to go

find out who had entered. To my surprise, Asia stood in front of the donuts and coffee dancing. I knew she had those darn cordless earbuds like she always did. I didn't bother calling out to her because she wouldn't hear me anyway. Instead, I went back to my desk to continue with my tasks. Shortly after, the rest of the crew trickled into the office.

CHAPTER 7

BISHOP WHITE

I USED to run the streets and made so much money that I needed accountants to keep track of my shit. As a rehabilitated member of society, I've changed my ways. Out of the drug game, I owned a barbershop and realized living legit wasn't bad. I still had clout in the streets and found out what happened in the streets.

Raised by my grandmother, she taught me how to treat a woman with respect. She also taught me not to raise my voice or hand to a woman because it didn't solve anything. Then there were the thots and ignorant bitches that didn't deserve my respect. You might think I'm a harsh nigga, but I'm just brutally honest. If a chick can't respect herself, why should I? I had an issue with women, and I blamed my mom who gave up custody of my siblings and me. She had a drug issue, and before she split, she made sure Big Mama kept us close.

Before we moved in with my grandma permanently, my older sister Deja and I took care of the household and our younger brother Tariq. I hustled by selling drugs while she kept the house in order. I made sure they were fed and bathed and made sure they went to school. It was a harsh reality that we played the role of mom and dad instead of being kids ourselves. Everything happens for a reason, and our struggle taught me how to provide and survive.

With the odds stacked against me as a black man, I went to jail at the age of twenty-seven. My incarceration left my siblings in the care of Big Mama. Disgusted that my family suffered the consequences from my actions, I made a plan to change for them, myself, and other young boys. When I was released, it turned out in my favor, and within a few months, my sister helped me open a barbershop. Everything was legit with paperwork and all.

I lived alone in my bachelor pad, where I cooked, cleaned, sewed, and took care of my own shit. With an unreliable dope head for a mother, I learned at an early age how to be a man and take care of the home. The streets taught me things about life a woman couldn't do, but I take my hat off to my granny. She was a true definition of a strong black woman. Tariq and I were taught by my grandmother how to keep a house and hold our own as men just in case of married or settled down. Being single it was hard to find a serious woman on my level who didn't play games. Then I met Erika Cain.

I met Erika at the All White Affair. She immediately caught my attention from the moment she drove up. Little mama was pushing a white Lexus and stepped out that bitch dripping in sauce. When we came in closer proximity, I got a better glimpse of her seductive brown eyes. Before the sexual thoughts popped inside my head, I felt chills run through me. She was beautiful. When I approached her inside the building, I tried to play it cool in case she shot me down. To my surprise, she engaged in conversation, and that night, I learned a lot of interesting things about her. For the first time in a long time, I had finally met a woman worth pursuing. A few days afterward, shorty remained on my mind. So naturally, I set in motion a plan to get to know her better.

Impressed that Erika ran a nonprofit organization that helped women and kids spoke volumes about her reputation and character. I loved that she made it a mission to give back. That turned me on more than a half-naked bitch that would let me fuck for a value meal at McDonald's. She was more than a pretty face. She had the whole package and liked to have fun. Thick in all the right places, she didn't take shit to heart, and I liked that about her.

Erika was a different breed from these other chicks in the streets with her nonchalant attitude. She was the only woman that I felt an attraction to and connected with intellectually. I wanted to get at her in a sexual way too, but I was trying to build a friendship first. We met in August, and everything about her screamed go-getter. On that grown woman shit, she remained humbled, and she didn't act stuck up.

Once we exchanged digits and chatted a few times, I invited her to kick it with a few of my folks and me. We had food, drinks, and played games at Dave & Buster's had been the perfect way to observe her interactions with my sister Deja and my homie Chico. To my surprise, everybody kicked it and had pure fun. Any woman who could get along with Deja and Chico possessed magical power because they didn't like anybody.

The more we hung out alone, the more I felt some type of way but didn't know how to tell her. It had only been a month of knowing each other, but I wanted her bad. Resistance had been something I had to practice anytime we hooked up. Besides, self-respect wasn't something a lot of chicks possessed in this day in age. I've seen all types of women in my lifetime. Erika walked to the beat of her own drum, and she had become intoxicating to me.

My boy Chico hit my line to let me know he was on his way to my crib. His ass was never on time, so I sat a little longer until he knocked on the door. It was a surprise that nigga was awake before noon let alone on time.

"Dawg, we ain't gotta hit your barbershop. These bitches are going for the scruffy look anyway. I don't even care, bro."

"Hell yeah. A young cat came in the shop the other day to get lined up and showed me a group on Facebook. It was nothing but niggas with beards and shit. It fucked my head up."

"Yes, nigga, these women out here wildin' out over beards, dawg. I had to pop this bitch's hand yesterday for trying to touch my shit," Chico commented.

"Damn, it's a movement, huh." I chuckled while I sat watching him talk.

Chico had been my nigga from way back when and ran the streets with me, but he went clean too. Now that nigga worked for the sausage factory and fucked around with bitches while his girlfriend Antoinette remained faithful. Despite his ways, he was my dude, and one I trusted like a brother. I was the type of nigga who kept shit real, and I called him out when in the wrong. I tried to warn him of the dangers of having a side chick and main chick. I tried to warn him occasionally that juggling women were bad. When his ass was laid in the hospital like Martin in the movie *Thin Line Between Love and Hate*, he'll be satisfied.

We ended up going to my shop so that I could touch him up with a lining and trim. Once he left, I cleaned the utensils and sanitized everything before closing up. Early in the evening, I hit Erika line while I got inside the car.

"Hey, what's up Erika? Are you busy right now?"

"Hey, Bishop, what's good? I'm just sitting around blowing back. Why?"

"We should go catch a movie and get you out of the house for a few hours. You down?"

"Aye, I wanted to see that movie with my Taraji P and Idris Elba," she insisted.

"I could pick you up at nine o'clock. We could go to the Marcus Majestic Cinema for the ten o'clock show." All of a sudden, it grew silent before she finally responded.

"Umm... How about I meet you at the theater? I like to drive myself."

"Oh, excuse me, Miss Independent," I joked.

"My bad. It's just that I'd feel more comfortable if you didn't know where I live. Men nowadays are a bit psycho. No offense," she clarified.

"None taken," I lied but understood her position. "Well, text me when you are on the way out. I at least want to watch out for you."

"Cool. I'll see ya in a little bit."

"Aiight. Peace."

―――

In the parking lot, trying not to look suspicious or creepy, I patiently waited for Erika to roll up. I must have checked my watch ten times before she finally arrived. Although against her driving alone at night, I couldn't tell her what to do. I flicked my headlights twice as a sign so that she could park nearby. We greeted each other and walked inside for our tickets and snacks. Seated towards the back, we got comfortable while the previews played. I swear she had to be the finest redbone I've laid eyes on. I probably watched her more than the movie. Shit, her aura was intoxicating. Although a nigga didn't get any action, it was a breath of fresh air to be around Erika.

Things between the two of us had been going so smooth that I invited her to my crib to chill. I ordered food, we watched movies on Netflix, and smoked. Halfway through the second movie, my boy Chico hit me, but his ass had already been in the neighborhood. He didn't give me a chance to warn him about Erika being over. When he entered, it had been like any other time, but when he glanced at Erika, the vibe changed. *Did I miss something? I don't know why the hell they mugging each other*, I thought shrugging it off.

Chico stuck around for another ten minutes before he dipped out. After that, I noticed the slight change in Erika who had gone from smiley to resting bitch face mode. Not sure how to proceed, I let the evening play out careful not mentioning my observations.

━━━

I allowed a week pass by before I reached out to Erika in hopes she would join me for dinner or something. She texted back saying she had her hands tied with her organization. I understood she had a business to handle, so I accepted and respected her for it. However, she continued to use the same reason, which was a sign she had been ghosting me. I felt some type of way because she had grown on me. Not trying to appear desperate, I hit her up two more times before saying fuck it.

Later in the week Erika called me asking to stop over for a minute to chat about something important. That type of language only meant she wanted to let me down in person. For some reason I grew upset because women always played with men's emotions. I had a few drinks while I waited for her to arrive. Within half an hour the sound of the doorbell rang throughout the house. It prompted me to swiftly head towards the door to let her inside.

"Damn girl you look in anything you wear. Come in." I gazed at her as she entered. She had dressed down in a red Adidas jogging suit, hair slicked back in a ponytail.

I followed behind her imagining what it would be like to tap that yellow ass. She made herself comfortable by sitting in the lounge chair. I watched Erika's gaze ping-ponged as she avoided direct eye contact.

"Why are you acting different?" I questioned.

"I'm not," she quickly answered. She then flashed a fake smile.

"Now I know you bulling." I poured another drink then took a seat across from her so we could clear the air.

"I just want to make sure there are no hard feelings between us. It was fun hanging out but we wouldn't work out as a couple. Not to mention, Chico and Deja."

Before I knew it, we begin to spit words back and forth. If words were visible, it would've looked like daggers flying across the room. The more she talked shit, the hotter I got, not to mention I hadn't fucked in a minute. Then she had the nerve to bring my sister's name into the shouting match. That's when I really got pissed because family was off limits. All of a sudden I raised my left hand and slapped her across the face.

"Nigga what the fuck is wrong with you?"

"Ain't shit wrong, you the one playing with a nigga emotions. I thought we had something," I yelled.

"Something is definitely wrong with you for putting hands on me," she snapped.

I watched as Erika held her face with a grimace look that turned into anger. Automatically I regretted what I did but it was no turning back. A woman with a flip lip turned my switch to black.

"It only takes one time for a person to show their true colors. You are dead to me." Erika slapped the glass from my hand in motion for the door.

"Huh, all you yellow bitches are the same, stuck up. Get the hell on," I yelled out.

Erika stuck up her middle finger then slapped my door as hard as she could. All I could do was shake my head and clean up the glass that had shatter on the floor. I hit Chico line afterwards. I knew he would help me forget the shit with Erika.

CHAPTER 8

TYREE LYONS

ON THE ROAD for a few weeks at a time, Erika and I kept in touch whenever possible. I went from Chicago to Baltimore and back to Wisconsin, each time adopting a different persona. Erika became my female friend. She was loyal and cool as fuck. She was like me, broken and in need of love, but too scared to trust anyone. Held up in the Edgewater Hotel room in Madison, I had an eye on my target until he checked in next door. A white man in his late forties who skipped out on a ten thousand dollar tab, my job was to take him out quick. Unfortunately, I lost my visual of him for almost twenty-four hours, which nearly fucked up the hit. Thankfully his nightly urge to see naked women prompted his visit Club Pussue`.

My military background trained me on how to sneak up on a target without being detected. Dressed in black like a thief in the night, the opportunity finally came. The sooner the deed was done, I would be free to take a day or two off. Parked a few cars away in the parking lot, I had to wait for the right moment to catch him sauced up. Shortly after eleven o'clock, my target stumbled out the doors with his shirt untucked. While he made it towards the parking lot, I exited from my vehicle and moved swiftly to his car. I slipped on a pair of latex gloves before I touched any part of his car. His dumb ass didn't lock up, so I eased in his back seat and softly closed the door. Imagine his reaction when I appeared in the rearview mirror.

"Buddy, I hope you had fun tonight because it's your last night! You have money to throw at dancers, but you must have forgotten your debts to Fat Tony."

"Shit! Shit! Shit! Aye man, please tell Fat Tony I'll pay him. Some shit came up and I—" he tried to explain, but I cut him off.

"It's too late now, dude. He doesn't even want the money now. It's about principle and you keeping your word. You failed to do what you promised, so now you must pay with your life."

"Oh no, please don't do this man. I'm sorry that shit didn't go as planned."

"Look, I don't want to do this, but I have specific orders that must be followed. Don't worry. I'll get this over quickly. Do you have any last words?"

"I fucked up big time," he mumbled as the sound of remorse trailed through his voice.

"We all fuck up from time to time and must deal with the consequences of our actions. This, my friend, is your consequence," I lectured.

I quickly wrapped the seat belt around his neck and literally choked the life out of him. No longer breathing after a few seconds, I unwrapped the polyester strap from around him. His head leaned on the headrest slightly to the left. I bent down and used my left hand to feel for the lever to let the seat back. I slid out the car, looked in both directions, and quietly closed the door. On the way back to my ride, I took off my gloves careful to discard them.

Relieved to complete another task, I went back to Edgewater Hotel to shower and smoke. Each kill was different from one another ended in the same result, money in the bank. Sheltered from the world except for work purposes life had been a repetitive never-ending saga. At times I wondered how long could I go on taking lives until it's my turn to face the reaper. The dark and evil thoughts that tended to fill my head ceased whenever Erika and I talked. However, this particular conversation made me tense.

When I talked to Erika, she told me she met this nigga named Bishop. It pissed me off because I didn't want her talking to another dude. Regardless of our status, the thought of another nigga around her wasn't cool. All of a sudden, the name rang a bell, and I realized he was on my hit list. Bishop owed debt from years ago and other reasons that had nothing to do with me.

———

I got back in town a night later, and Erika's house was my first stop. It couldn't have been coincident that dude happened to pop up. I needed answers before he caught my bullet. Not sure how Erika would react, I planned to stay calm with her no matter what.

"I need to know more about this nigga Bishop, and please don't leave out any details," I ordered.

Erika raised her eyebrows and asked, "Is this for business or a personal reason you need to know?"

"It's both. Do yourself a favor and leave buddy alone."

"And you know this because?" she inquired me.

"Because I am a summons server and he has a record." It

hurt to sit and tell her a partial truth. In my profession, instead of serving legal documents, I served death.

I did my best to explain to her the severity of the situation without revealing what I did for a living. It was best not to disclose that information yet. We chatted a little longer about the situation as she tried to make her case for why I shouldn't worry. She even accused me of being jealous, but it didn't faze me. Once our disagreement ceased, we smoked and laughed for the rest of the night.

Burning the midnight oil, I used my downtime to take my guns apart to clean. Bishop had been on my mind, and it bothered me that Erika continued to talk to him. It wasn't out of jealousy, but for her safety, I didn't want to run up and kill him while she was with him. Bishop had become an enemy, which meant anyone tied to him was also the enemy. The bounty on his head came from some unsettled business while he was in prison.

To learn more about my target and his habits, I began my daily stakeouts on his whereabouts, folks he hung out with, and where he laid his head at night. From surveillance software, I learned that his sister Deja was the eldest. She was also his right hand and her brother's keeper. Although she was a female, it didn't mean she couldn't be on the enemy hit list.

Against my advice, Erika continued to see that chump Bishop and as much as I tried to play hard, I got in my feelings. Imagine my surprise to see her out at Dave & Buster's with him a few other folks. She just didn't understand how much restraint it took to keep me from going inside to snatch her up. Instead, I chilled in the car and patiently waited until the crew exited and headed to their vehicles. A few cars behind, I trailed them until I saw Erika get home safely.

Damn this girl got me feeling like a damn stalker and shit. What the fuck are you doing Tyree? I thought as I parked near her condo.

Once I came to my senses, I pulled off and took my ass home for the night. My repetitive routine after a job consisted of food, shower, and a perfectly rolled blunt. Alone in my king sized bed, I watched *The Man in 3B* on Netflix. That movie had some crazy twists but turned out to be a good flick. It prompted me to call E just to hear her voice. Not sure if she'd pick up, I only intended to let it ring three times.

"How did you know I was still awake, night owl?" she asked in a joking manner.

"I didn't honestly. I just figured I'd try and here we are. What you up to?"

"Just put my smoke out, now I'm chilled back enjoying the buzz. And you?"

"Same. Just finished a movie on Netflix. The shit was crazy but good. I couldn't stop thinking about you either. What did you do today?"

My question intended to test her honesty. I wanted to know if she would lie or tell the truth. It was one of many tests for women. I needed to know where we stood if our friendship would turn into something else.

"Umm... You won't like it, but I decided to hang with Bishop and his folks at Dave & Buster's. It turned out to be a good time. I know how you feel about the situation, so we can change topics."

"Oh. You know what I'm cool. I just need you to be careful. You're a grown ass woman so I can't forbid who you see." Erika had just passed my test. I loved how she kept it real instead of lying.

"I promise to watch my back, and I'll let you know if I run into trouble. Now if you don't mind, my eyelids getting heavy by the minute. Thank you for checking in on me. Chat with you tomorrow."

"Alright, ma. Sleep well, and try not to dream about me too much."

"Cocky ass nigga! Night Tyree," she remarked.

"Night baby," I commented and disconnected the call.

CHAPTER 9

ERIKA CAIN

TALKING to Tyree on the phone was weird at first, but it became a regular thing. We talked more than we hung out since his ass was always on the road. Not yet a couple or anything I felt the need to be honest with him about meeting another guy. Not sure how he felt about me, I wanted to be upfront about mine to avoid miscommunication between us. My confession about chilling with Bishop didn't seem to sit well with him. He indicated he would explain once we were face to face again. I hoped he wouldn't be that jealous type of dude.

As promised, Tyree showed up at my door, and oddly, I was glad to see him. I invited him in, and he made his way to the couch. As I sat down on the other end of the couch, I'll admit I grew nervous. We looked each other over with a few glances before he began to talk.

"Ms. Erika Cain, you look gorgeous as usual!"

"Thanks. You're looking handsome as shit yourself."

"So what's up with this Bishop cat? I need all the details too."

"I met him, he seemed interesting enough to chat with,

and we exchanged numbers. That is basically all. Please don't tell me you are one of those guys?"

"What the jealous type? The man who doesn't want you having male friends? Naw, I'm the protective type, the man who only wants the best for you. That nigga is no good."

"How do you know?"

"All you need to know is what I'm telling you is the truth. Dude is bad news, but I understand if you don't believe me. Just know I got your back no matter what."

"Well, thank you for your concern, really, but I'll be fine. It's not like I plan to marry that nigga."

"Alright, I'll leave it alone but know I got yo back. You wanna blow one?"

"Hell yeah! Let me grab us something to drink while you twist up. Make yourself comfortable."

We spent the rest of the evening high, laughing and flirting with each other. Deep down, I knew something about him would eventually make me give up the goods to him.

Upon my further interest in Bishop, our communication and interactions increased. He was supposed to keep me company when Tyree was out of town. Down to earth and opposite of Tyree, he made me laugh. There was some sexual tension between us. However, I tried to meet him in public places. As much as I wanted to jump his bones, my panties were only coming off for Tyree.

Only in the first phase of knowing each other, Bishop could only be a distant memory. The beard game was one reason I even decided to talk to him. Nevertheless, we smoked and chilled whenever my work allowed me to be away. As time progressed, Bishop brought his sister and homeboy around me, which was a sign he was too comfortable with me. As a female, I knew when another female felt a type of way towards me. Our first meet and greet took place at Dave & Buster's. Everything was cool while we sipped drinks, ate, and played games. Laughs and fun lead me to believe his people were cool.

Shit went so smooth that when Bishop asked me out to the movies, I accepted his offer. He tried to be as respectful and cool, which were good qualities in a man. The solo time alone wasn't too bad. However, Tyree had surfaced to the top of my mind. To avoid drama, I decided to continue meeting up with Bishop for innocent dates. I'll admit that I had a few sexual urges whenever we were together, but I knew better than to fuck him. Besides, I had been saving my goodies for Tyree.

The next encounter happened on Sunday evening while at Bishop's home. He ordered pizza, wings, and rolled a couple of blunts. Netflix and chilling minus sex was the only thing jumping when Chico stopped by. From the time his peanut head ass entered the door until he left the shady looks that he threw at me left me stunned. Why was he so threatened by me? I hadn't done anything bogus to him or Bishop. Instead, of being petty, I finished my food, lit my blunt, and shot dirty stares right back.

After hanging around for half an hour, he left. It wasn't until then I realized shit would never work out with Bishop. Although we had a good time, my inner self just didn't feel him anymore. Chico seemed like the type of dude I'd have to kill. His vibe bothered me. From there, I had to figure out a way to tell Bishop my interests have changed. Unable to figure out the perfect way to let him down, I kept my distance for a few days.

━━━

With a clouded mind, I decided to indulge in some shopping with Keisha in Chicago. She drove, and I treated for our spa and food. We found sale after sale at Nordstrom, Neiman Marcus, Rue 21, Bath, and Body Works. Amid laughter, a pecan brown skin man with almond-shaped eyes stared Keisha down. He stared at her so hard that I thought his eyes would pop out his head. In the Apple store to check out the iPads, he stood across the room, and it made me feel a bit uneasy. Keisha ass wasn't paying attention, but my antennas stood straight up.

"Girl, that guy over there by the phones has been gawking at you. His creepy looking ass better not come over here either. Are you buying anything?"

"Probably not, let's go grab some food now. Ooh, we should go to The Capital Grille."

"Let's put these bags in the car first!"

We walked out of the high ass Apple store and headed back through the mall and exited the door closest to the vehicle. I searched inside my Michael Kors purse for my phone as I walk alongside Keisha. A few feet from the car, the topic changed to Tyree out the blue. Keisha seemed to be fishing for something with her questions.

"Tyree seems cool, but he's so secretive and anti-social."

"Yeah. He is a little blunt and straightforward, but he has another side. Life for him growing up was a bitch. He doesn't really do people like that."

"What does he do for a living?" Keisha probed.

"His job requires him to travel a lot. He is a jack of all trade," I answered, not revealing too much information.

"Hum," she sounded.

Not sure where Keisha was going with the line of questioning, I stopped walking to inquire what she meant. "What's that supposed to mean?" I questioned her with raised eyebrows.

"Nothing. All I'm going to say is be careful," she warned.

"Thanks for your concern Keisha, but it's all good. I'll be fine. Anyway, enough about my life, what's going on your way?"

"Shit, working and improving my craft at Nails and Spa. Can you believe I've been there for six months already? Girl, you wouldn't believe the shit I overhear on a daily basis. Those women were in there telling all their business."

"I bet gossiping ass ladies. What types of stuff have you heard?"

"I found out what's going on in the streets, which is fucking who and damn near anything you name it."

"Speaking of, who is the lucky man these days in your life? And don't leave out any details," I voiced, giving her the side look.

Upon entering Capital Grille, Keisha began to fill me in and mentioned the name Chico. I almost jumped out my skin, unsure if it was Bishop's friend Chico. Once seated, I probed a little more, and just as I thought it was the same guy. The waiter wasted no time getting us drinks and taking our orders.

"The only dilemma is his girlfriend Antoinette. All of us went to high school together; Chico even took me to prom. Shit kind of just happened, now we're slipping around whenever we can."

Surprised by Keisha's confession I held my criticizing comments unsure what to say in response. Although her comments made me wonder, I refused to cast judgement because she had been a friend. My first mind told me not to share certain information with Keisha just in case she became my arch enemy. She continued on as I retrieved my phone scanning the screen, I had been waiting for a message from Tyree.

"Speak of the girlfriend," Keisha hissed.

"What?" I raised my head to find Keisha staring towards the exit at a woman who sat nearby. Right away I frowned unconsciously; she was too pretty to be with Chico ugly ass. Quickly I fixed my face and leaned forward.

"Do you think she knows or it's just pure coincidence?" Keisha's eyes darted back and forth.

"What you going to do if she spots ya?" I questioned. Curious how the situation would play out, I minded my business as I watched the woman.

"Say hello, shit," Keisha joked.

Just then the waiter approached carefully placing our plates down in front of us. Ready to enjoy my meal, I licked my lips not wasting time. I dug my fork into the saucy pasta shells anticipating Alfredo sauce. I tried hard not to stare at Antoinette but my seat faced her direction. The vibration of my phone caused me to quickly jump in my seat.

"Girl, what the hell wrong with you?"

"It's my phone," I laughed.

Before I could open his message my cheeks spread from excitement. He had become my favorite notification. I raised the phone in front of me to type back to him. In the process, I also snapped a picture and captioned it Chico's girlfriend. Of course, I revealed what I learned to Tyree just because we had grown close. He had slowly become my BFF who I shared all the gossip with. The remainder of our meal went without incident thankfully because my ass was too full and old to be fighting. Tyree came by later that night once he finished with work.

CHAPTER 10

CHICO HAWKINS

IN THE CLUB having a good time, this badass chick quickly distracted me. I sat in my chair at the bar as she stood and waited for the bartender. With a constant gaze of her body and face, and she looked familiar. Her hair was in an updo style, so I was able to see her facial features, and she was attractive in the face. Most bitches have tight bodies, but they faces be busted. Anyway, I leaned in to run my game, and surprisingly, she took the bait. Once the bartender came our way, I caught his attention.

"Aye, can I get a Jack and Coke and whatever the lady wants? Keep my tab open please," I requested.

In no time, he got our drinks. With her attention now, she turned my way long enough to make eye contact with me. I couldn't believe my eyes. It was an old classmate of mines from high school, and she still looked the same. I couldn't believe my eyes.

"Damn! Keisha, is that you or are my eyes deceiving me?"

"Oh my goodness, this is crazy! Chico, I can't believe I ran into you. How have you been doing?"

"Shit, I won't complain. A nigga got a legal job living this thing called life."

"I was actually thinking about you last week. I saw Mario too, but you were always my favorite in school," she added.

She took a few sips of her Long Island Ice Tea and moved closer to me. We continued our conversation over the background noise that didn't completely drown our voices out. Fifteen minutes later, she was chatty Cathy and loosened up. I could tell she was more relaxed by her body language and the extra touching she did. I pulled her close and put my hand around her waist, to whisper in her ear.

"You want to change the scenery and go somewhere less crowded?" I questioned hoping that she'd say yes. I was horny, and Keisha looked extra good.

"Why not, I don't have any other plans tonight," she answered.

Music to my ears, we exited the establishment, both of us extra touchy when we walked outside to my car. I could tell she wanted to fuck. We couldn't go to my crib because of my girl, Netta, so we went to the hotel to rekindle the high school flame we shared.

She didn't waste time undressing the second our hotel door closed. Keisha popped that pussy on me, and even though it was wrong, that shit felt right as hell. As I hit that shit from the back, high school memories flooded my head. Sweat continued to ripple down my chest as I long dicked her thrust after thrust. Her pussy muscles contracted around my pole, causing me to pull out.

"Hell naw, I can't cum yet. Flip over on your back!" I ordered. She did as told as my eyes zeroed in on them titties practically salivating.

Her beautiful pussy stared me in the face. I ran my

tongue across it like it was chocolate ice cream. Without further hesitation, I slid all seven inches inside her. The harder I pounded, the more we began to breathe heavily, almost reaching our climax.

In my arms, Keisha had a hold of me since age seventeen, and I just couldn't shake her. The worst part of it all, Netta knew about my history with Keisha.

"Aye, you remember prom night?

"Do I? Shit, that's the first time you gave me a taste of your sweet love. That's when life was fun." We spent the remainder of our time fucking, eating, and reliving our high school memories.

It had been a week since I spent time with Keisha. Our encounter turned from friendly to sexual and got wild. My problem was making sure my girl never found out because she would flip the fuck out. In need of advice, I went to my boy Bishop's barbershop to spill my guts to him over a lineup. He had a grand opening yesterday, so I had to come to support him. I walked through the doors and liked what I saw because Bishop was doing something positive with his life. The shop was clean, and everything was brand new. He had five male barbers and three females who were skilled in hair and nails.

"Hey man, I'm digging the place," I said as I gave Bishop a handshake.

"Look what the cat dragged in. Nice to see your brother, welcome to my new spot. You like it?" he asked.

"It's really nice my nig, and I wanted to support you by getting a lineup and shit. I need to holla at you about a woman problem I'm having. A playa got two chicks, and I can't decide on what to do. Netta's my rider and heart, but I ran into Keisha from high school."

"Keisha with the perfect, round ass and pretty face? Damn, man, I understand your struggle," he said and laughed.

"Man, I ran into her at the club about a week ago, and messed around and took her the hotel room. She is a straight up freak, dawg. Now I have the urge to see her, but my girl is suspicious, and I'm not trying to piss her off."

My phone rung as I chatted with my boy, and to my surprise, it was Keisha. I answered the phone in my cool dude voice.

"Aye, what's up with you, girl? I was actually just thinking about you!"

"Is that so? I'm not on shit, just came from the grocery store and paid a few bills. What you on right now?" she asked. Her voice was soft and the perfect pitch unlike them annoying high-pitched chicks.

"I'm getting faded at the moment, why what's up?"

"I wanted to see if you wanted to hook up later? I've dreamed about that dick and want more. Will you give it to me?"

This girl was a freak and was now hooked on my jerky stick. I wanted to get inside her again too. "Hell yeah, we can work something out. Let me hit you back when I leave the shop. Talk soon." I ended the call and smiled like I was the man.

"Nigga, she's begging for the D again," I said to Bishop.

"Dog, you a fool, my nigga. Yo ass better be careful and watch out for Netta," he advised, and I knew he was right.

"Yeah, I got this, and after this time, I have to leave Keisha alone. It's time to make some changes, but her pussy is my weakness, nigga," I said and laughed.

Changing the topic, I wanted to see how shit was popping his way with that new chick. Unable to look him in the face due to the clippers at my head. "Aye, what's up with that yellow chick Erika?"

"Man little mama's a pistol, shit I love everything about her so far, but she ain't been hitting a nigga back ever since the day you popped up. I don't know what transpired, but she's been curving a nigga."

"Well, I don't trust her. Maybe shit worked out for the best. Either way, be careful, it's something about her," I warned.

"Nigga, you the last person who need to be lecturing me on trust but good looking out."

"Word." I laughed, but in the pit of my stomach, a gnawing feeling ate at me. Bishop hooked me up, and I paid him and stepped out of the chair. "Keep up the good work, my nig. We certainly need to chop it up over drinks. Until then, keep it real and holla at a playa."

We shook hands, and I walked out the door back to my car. Something in the male DNA wouldn't allow me to be monogamous. Bishop always tried to warn me about my ways with his philosophical viewpoints. His exact words *"Heed my warning bro, these women gonna fuck you up one day,"* echoed in the back of mind as I leaned back in my seat and dialed Keisha.

"That didn't take long at all!"

Her sensual voice made me forget everything Bishop said as my dick jumped. "Damn, you sound sexy. I'm fresh from the barbershop and just wanted to hit you back as I promised. What are you doing?"

"Chilling at the crib eating pineapples and watching *Shottas* with Ky-Mani Marley fine dread headed ass. Are you coming over?"

"That nigga ain't got shit on me. You already know that. Hell yeah, I'm coming over, and then we both gonna cum. Be ready to get this D the second I get there."

"Oh, wow, there you go. You're one cocky ass nigga. I hope you know that shit. Oh, don't worry, I'll be waiting for you to come to dick me down."

"On my way!"

The call disconnected, and I drove to her spot ready to fuck the dog shit out of her. When it came to sex, I didn't waste time and gave a chick my best stroke game. Keisha made me work harder for the prize, but her sweet, gushy stuff was worth every ripple of sweat, thrust, and lick.

Less than twenty minutes later, I was at the door with my man at full attention, ready to get inside that warm lady garden. Pussy made a nigga risk it all like a game of Russian roulette, the price to pay never seemed clear until it's too late. Whenever I was with Keisha, the world around me didn't matter.

I didn't have to knock. She greeted me at the door wearing a pair of boy shorts with a white crop top and no bra. When she turned around, I was so hypnotized by her ass. It was such a beautiful thing, like a perfectly shaped peach. Her ass was so perfect; it's a shame she had such a weapon.

"Ummmm! Girl you look good enough to eat right now. I hope you prepared to get that back blown out. My shit hard as a brick but first I have a taste for your sweet nectar."

"I'm all in for it, baby! Follow me if you dare to have your world rocked upside down."

"You ain't said nothing but a word," I shot back as I slapped her right cheek.

From there it was on like donkey kong. I didn't waste any time stripping her out of her bottoms so that I could dive my tongue into that sweet, gushy stuff.

Every sexual act we did in that room made my decision to cheat again easier regardless of that little voice in the back of my head. Whenever Keisha was in my presence, I lit up from the inside out. I didn't know what it was about her pussy, but that shit made me go stupid each time I got a dose.

Keisha lay on my chest sweaty and all, and I loved every minute without a doubt. The rapid speed of my heartbeat finally slowed down, and my breathing returned to its normal state. She used her right hand and fingers to glide lightly against my stomach sending chills through my body.

"Girl you took all my damn energy, but it was worth every drop of sweat and thrust. I gave you my all."

"My legs are still numb, and my vajayjay is throbbing, so I'd say you did the job."

"My whole body is limp now," I joked. The sound of her phone vibrating interrupted the moment.

"My bad," she apologized while she leaned over to grab it. "Oh, it's my girl Erika. I'll hit her up later.

"Light skinned with long hair?" I couldn't help but inquire since it probably was the same chick Bishop had been talking to.

"Yeah, why?" She had a slight frown on her face trying to figure out how I knew her friend.

"I met her at my boy Bishop's house, that's all. Nothing to worry about, now let me play them titties," I joked.

I took her soft nipple in between my fingers until it grew hard and erect. A few squeezes of Keisha's soft breasts had me practically watering at the mouth for a sweet treat. All of the sex I had with Keisha had been mind-blowing. My actions were definitely bogus, and Netta never deserved it, but I knew she wouldn't find out. I made sure to cover my tracks and never worried. Keisha was my little secret.

━━━

Netta didn't have a habit of going through my phone, but women were sneaky. I played it careful and put Keisha's number under the name K-Dog. After our run in, we picked up where we left off. I met up with Keisha on scheduled days, and we sent each other texts from time to time. Unable to leave Keisha alone, she had a spell over me. Incredible would be the one word used to describe how she made me feel. Netta trusted me, but I continuously cheated and fucked up.

Shit had been good on the home front and at work. The weekends Netta and I chilled together since we both were off. She and I had been together for a few years, long enough to know each other's habits and shit. She had been a good woman, yet I repaid her with my dog ways. Old enough to know right from wrong, I was probably like other dudes who cheated— dumb. One of my weaknesses was pussy, particularly, from Keisha and Netta. I truly cared about Netta without a doubt, even though my actions contradicted that.

The following weekend, Netta and I planned to spend time alone together, we did just that too. After movies and food, she hinted that she wanted to get busy in the bedroom. She grabbed between my legs, giving my junk a gentle squeeze.

"Damn girl, you something else," I tried to get excited.

The truth is, Keisha had worn my dick out, I only had a few good strokes left. I played shit cool and did my best to give her what she wanted. In motion, I tried my hardest to get her off before she cussed me out. It took longer to concentrate since a nigga had been burnt out from sex. As soon as Netta dug her nails into the lower part of my back, my shit got hard enough to finish.

"Ahhh," she moaned.

"Sorry baby," I apologized, while I climbed off the top of her. She then rushed to the bathroom to handle her business before returning. Once she returned and slid under the covers, I headed for the bathroom. Afterward, we passed the hell out.

———

Sunday morning, when we woke up, my morning wood game had me ready to fuck the shit out of Netta. To wake her, I rubbed up against her so that she could feel me. I had to make up for the night before. In a slow motion, her hand reached towards me, and I felt her hand connect with my meat.

"Good morning," she mumbled.

"Hey, boo! You ready for some of this lovin' girl?" I joked.

Already naked, I slid inside her while she lay on her side. Somehow, with each stroke, my mind went back to the last time I fucked Keisha. All of a sudden, my concentration went left, and then my dick went soft again. I tried to play that shit off by rushing to the bathroom. When I came out, Netta had sat up with her face glued to her phone. I knew then she was about to curse my ass out.

CHAPTER 11

ANTOINETTE NIXON

FINALLY FINISHED WITH MY SHIFT, I clocked out and got the hell out of the building without looking back. Glad to see Friday, my ass was tired. Being a supervisor at Walmart had its benefits, but them damn employees were something else. I hopped in my car so that fast you would've thought somebody was after me. A fifteen-minute drive felt more like five when I pulled into the driveway next to Chico's car. When my feet walked through the threshold of the front door, Chico had made it down a few stairs to greet me. Shirtless wearing jogging pants instantly made me clench my pussy.

"Hey, baby! You are wearing the hell out of those joggers. That dick print is impressive," I commented. He smirked all proud like because that D game was on point.

"Come get some if you bad," he teased.

Of course, I locked the door and headed up the stairs in his direction towards our bedroom. After a quick shower, Chico gave me the best body massage literally from head to toe. Both a frontal and back made my body feel brand new.

Then he slightly parted my legs and gently played with me. Eyes closed, it felt like his fingers were dancing causing orgasm after another.

Suddenly I felt him slide inside of me, sending a warm tingling feeling through my body. In and out, his dick felt so good, and it calmed the ache I had down there. For five years he has fucked me so well and caused me to catch the dick happy syndrome these other crazy ass chicks caught. I wrapped my legs around him as we both slow grind, letting our bodies do what came naturally. Once he itched my scratch and we climaxed, he slid out just in time as the condom was almost off. Yes, we used condoms at all times despite our long history together.

Not perfect by far, our relationship had been a complicated one, but he was all I had. Most of my family were either dead or in jail, and that included my mama and dad. Let's just say the family business didn't turn out to be as lucrative as they thought. I, on the other hand, basically had to raise myself, so when Chico and I met, we grew very close. Still relatively young when we got serious, he taught me a few things. However, the lack of guidance from a mother resulted in my lack of knowledge on some shit.

By the next weekend, my body felt off. Something had been different from Chico lately. It just didn't seem like old times, and it bugged the hell out of me. It almost seemed as if his mind became detached. Then by accident, I found out the reason for his lack of attention. Usually, whenever his phone rang or beeped, I tended to mind my business, but something urged me to be nosy that particular time. When he went to the bathroom, my female intuition meter went nuts. Without touching one button, I leaned over across the bed and saw a picture of a topless woman displayed on the screen. An instant frown came over my face, and my mouth gaped open.

The small tattoo of a blue butterfly on the upper breast area was something I'd seen before. A flashback from high school automatically made me remember Keisha "slut bucket" Dixon. She used to always flaunt her ass and sets around the school. She and Chico had history, and I didn't have an issue, the past was just that. However, she crossed the line when she sent the picture, and Chico's ass wasn't any better. He was stupid enough to think he could keep a secret from me. When the bathroom door opened, I remained calm and sat on my side as if nothing had ever happened.

"Baby, your phone made a beeping sound several times." I held my phone in hand and scrolled on Facebook.

"It's probably nothing. It might've been Bishop hitting me back or something."

Without a peep, I continued to swipe my thumb across the screen while Chico got back in the bed next to me. That fool had no clue he was busted. I watched his facial reaction to the picture on his screen, that nigga blinked triple time. He then quickly glanced my way only to catch me staring a hole in his ass.

"Aye, blinky Bill you alright over there?"

"Yeah. It was one of those junk email pop-ups with some white chick flashing her titties."

No longer able to hold the words that itched to fly from my mouth, I refused to let him lie to my face. "Nigga, you a damn lie!" I spat while we eyeballed each other down. "Why was it saved as K-Dog?"

"What are you talking about?" He tried to hit me with the confused and dumbfounded face.

"Those titties had a blue butterfly tattoo. We both know who the hell sent the picture. Keisha is the only female I know with the same tattoo, nigga. Come on with another lie. I dare you."

"It's not like that, Netta. She plays too much and does that shit on purpose," he tried to explain.

"Of course. She's a fucking woman! We act crazy to let y'all niggas know not to fuck over us. You men lay your head and dick in the beds of multiple women then complain. ACT RIGHT, NIGGA!"

I tossed my phone aside and climbed on top of him so that he could hear me loud and clear. For a minute, I transformed and acted like the chick Sky from *Black Ink Crew* as I threatened him.

"If I catch ya ass fucking with that bitch one more time, I will fuck you up! Please don't test me! I love yo' black ass, but I will leave you too!" hollered out in frustration.

"I'm sorry. I got weak, and temptation got the best of me, but I love you, girl."

He gripped my waist. I could feel his manhood grow harder as our eyes never left each other. My pussy throbbed, but I refused to give in yet although I eventually knew he'd win the battle.

"That bitch Keisha needs to be removed from your vocabulary and phone. I'm too good of a woman. I be damned you treat me like shit. I'm not the one, straight up."

"Okay, I'm done for real. Watch this," he said as he tapped and scrolled on his phone screen. He showed me the contact for Keisha and pressed edit and then scrolled to the bottom to delete it.

Of course, he smooth talked me, flipped me over, and

fucked the attitude away. Call me stupid or gullible, but he had me addicted. We both were stubborn and liked to be in charge. We were in a toxic relationship, but the sex was too good to let go. I never thought I'd find myself in a situation so complicated. Sunday morning, I cleaned up, changed clothes, and left for a few hours.

Different day same shit, Chico continued to run the streets and fuck around as if he didn't hear my words loud and clear. Instead of catching a case or forgiving him again, I switched shit around. On the edge of my bed, I sat and scrolled through my contact list down to the M's. I tapped Money's name and waited for him to answer. When I heard his voice say hello, I froze.

"Umm, Money?"

"The one and only," he replied. "This sounds like Antoinette."

"Yes. It's amazing you know my voice after all this time. How you been doing, friend?" A smile crept over my face.

"I won't complain, doll face. Living, working, and surviving. You?"

"I'm in a transition shall I say. Not to change my gender or nothing like that though," I clarified quickly. He laughed so hard, and I realized how weird my statement sounded.

"What I meant to say is that I'm in the process of transitioning out of a jacked up relationship. Anyway, while cleaning out a closet, pictures from back in the day popped out. Hence my call to catch up."

"Aye, meet me for drinks in a few hours at Hawk Bowl. We can chop it up in person. It's been way too long."

"Sounds like a plan. Let me get my ass off this phone and find something to wear. I'll hit you when I'm pulling off."

"Looking forward to it!"

If I didn't know any better, it felt like he had a big ass smile on his face when we hung up the phone. Excited, I went to my closet to find my black Michael Kors freakum dress. It had been a while since I last saw Money, so catching up was all I planned to do. Being in the presence of another man was good enough for me since my man couldn't keep his ass home. Fresh and dressed to comfort, I slipped my phone in my clutch. I got in the car, but before I drove off, I texted Money.

━━

Not knowing what to expect upon arriving at the bar, I walked inside confident and ready for a drink. I only wanted to chat and enjoy the company of an old friend. Imagine my surprise when a third party sat at the bar with him, a woman in particular. I played it cool, and I'm glad I did because his lady friend was beautiful and pleasant. Within a few minutes, one would've thought the three of us were closer than close. Minutes turned into hours, and after several Martini's and lots of laughs, I had forgotten all of my troubles.

Over drinks, I observed Money from head to toe, unable to believe how handsome he had looked. He wore a fresh low fade cut and had the smoothest creamy skin like peanut butter. The brotha was F-I-N-E just as I remembered him to be back in the day. My attention turned to Breya, who was a cute redbone, and her body was nice, tight, and plump in all the right places. She actually made me have a dyke moment, something I'd never thought about before. Nevertheless, I planned to enjoy the night, whatever it consisted of.

Tipsy from the Martinis, I let Money and his girl get me back to their house. Intrigued by their story, I wanted to know more because it made me horny. They made me feel welcomed right away by providing me bottled water.

"Have a seat. Can I offer you anything else?" Breya asked as she stood in front of me.

I tried to ignore the fact that her nipples were rock hard and visible through her shirt. That shit kind of got me wet and didn't know what the hell I was about to get into. I scanned the place and noticed how cozy and charming their place was. They both seemed happy and in a good space.

"Netta, you smoke?" Money held up a Ziploc bag full of weed.

My eyes grew wide for a moment, as this was all unexpected. I wanted to say no, but I shook my head up and down to nonverbally answer yes. I watched him roll two blunts while Breya put on music in the background then disappeared for a good fifteen minutes. When she returned, she wore a provocative see-through lace gown that exposed her perky breasts. Money cheesed hard as hell just like a typical horny nigga. At that moment, I realized I was about to have my first gay moment and experience with a woman.

Weed made me horny, and I knew once I hit the blunt, my inner freak would be unleashed. Never in life had I ever revealed to anyone my secret interest in women. I only liked breasts on women and had yet to use my tongue on a nice pair. Now was my chance to explore all I ever wanted.

Interrupted by my thoughts, Money spoke up. "Aye, Netta, I will let you get this one started since you are the guest of the evening.

I reach for the blunt and lighter to spark up. I took a few pulls as I made a few clouds in the air. I passed it to Money as Breya kept the rotation going and handed me another one. It had been a while since I smoked like that, and it felt good just to enjoy myself. Once the smoke had vanished, I fell into a comatose state. I sat back on the couch, my body loosened up, and the sensations took over. The weed made me feel like I had been shot up with the good shit from the hospital. Suddenly I felt a ticklish feeling in the palm of my hand. It was Breya using her fingers to rub my palm, and it was an amazing thing.

Her fingers moved up my arm to my breasts, and I embraced the feeling instead of fight it. When I turned my head, Money was sucking on Breya's right nipple. I slipped off my dress, bra, and let my titties hang and wanted in on the action. Breya took interest and turned her attention to me as she took my nipple in her mouth. Money to join in and took the other one in his mouth.

"Ahh, this shit feels sooooo good! I can't believe I'm doing this with y'all," I confessed. Having my tits sucked at the same time was the best feeling yet, and as it happened, I evaluated both of them. Breya was gentle as she tugged on my chocolate nipples while Money was rougher.

"Let's move this party to the king-sized bed. This is everything I thought it would be." Money stood in his boxers with his pole curved. He led the way as Breya, and I followed him to the back bedroom. Breya held my hand.

Seeing Money without clothes made me realize how real the situation was about to get. My body yearned for attention. I dared to explore my sexuality since Chico felt the need to live his life. It felt like I was a character in one of Zane's or Quardeay's erotic books.

The next morning I woke up shocked by how far things had gone twenty-four hours ago. In bed with two strangers, life on the wild side felt good for a change. Money was awake when my eyes opened, and I could only imagine what he had to say. To my surprise, we just laid and chatted like we had done this before.

For another half hour, we lay in each other's company, and it felt so good that I didn't want to leave. However, reality waited on me. I had to pry myself from the bed to get the day started. Apparently, I had too many drinks because it didn't dawn on me that my car was left in the parking lot of the bar. Money reminded me while he filled in the blanks of my memory.

In the living room, I searched for my cell phone and found it on the floor by the couch. When I hit the home button, I noticed Chico had called eight times. It was pitiful to see him sweat me, but it didn't matter. Disregarding his calls, I tapped on the Uber app to set up a ride back to the bar.

"Well, I just ordered an Uber. I had a good time. Thank you. We gotta do it again."

"An Uber? Cancel that shit. I'll take you to get your car. I gotta go to get cut up at the shop anyway."

Just like that, the two of us walked out to his car. I still felt a little weird after all of the shit we did. He tried to get me to talk during the ride, but in honesty, my mind drifted back to the sexual acts we committed. A smile remained on my face the entire time. In a daydream state during the drive, I never felt the car when it stopped moving. Money had to shove my arm to get my attention. We said our good-byes as I got out and closed the door behind.

Back to reality, I prepared to deal with Chico who I knew had been going crazy since I ignored his calls. For the first time, my walk of shame felt enjoyable in every way. Time away made me feel new confidence to finally live life. Overnight my attitude changed and Chico sure as hell didn't like it.

CHAPTER 12

KENTRELL "MONEY" GIPSON

WHEN AN OLD FRIEND called me out the blue, it was crazy how fast I recognized her voice. I had a thing for her, but she never wanted to move from friendship status. Instead, she dissed a nigga for a no good ass dude. Nevertheless, I was excited to hear from her because she was always the chick that got away. I wanted her so bad, but she turned me down every time. Antoinette, Netta for short, tended to be a bit over dramatic at times, but I liked my women that way.

On that particular night, I had plans to go to the bar with my lady Breya for a few drinks and grown folks music. We kept our relationship spicy by having threesomes every other month. Feeling lucky, I invited Netta to the club so that she could hang. My lifestyle was unique because it worked for me, and I didn't have to sneak around with different women. Breya was bisexual and didn't have a problem with our arrangement. She even suggested we take turns selecting the woman to satisfy our sexual needs. I felt like the luckiest man in the world because my life was peaceful and drama free.

At the bar, we waited for Netta to show up, and I was nervous about her reaction when she saw another woman here with me. I hoped to catch up and have a good time, followed by sexual adventures. I continuously scanned the area looking for her to approach us. That is when I heard a voice behind me, and I turned around to see a beautiful woman standing before me.

"Damn Money, it is good to see you again. You look the same as the last time we saw each other. Still fine as hell too," she said and then looked over at Breya.

"Netta, wow, you look amazing. I'm glad to see you too. This here is Breya, my lady. If possible, I would like to tell you about her and how we hooked up. She isn't here for drama either," I explained before she went all sista girl on me and snapped out.

With a puzzled look on her face, she sat down and raised her finger for the bartender. She ordered a Martini and didn't waste time asking questions.

"Okay so what am I witnessing here and how did it happen? Are you both in a serious relationship?"

I laughed and tried to find the easiest way to explain it to her without her getting uncomfortable. Her vibe made me believe she was cool and open to what I was about to tell her. My eyes never left hers. I needed to see her nonverbal while she listened.

"Two Christmases ago, Breya and I met through a mutual friend at a holiday party that included alcohol and other items. We ended up participating in a threesome, and I connected with Breya. I noticed she enjoyed it just as much as I did. We ended up hooking up several more times, and now here we are."

"That was a spontaneous and unexpected hookup story," Netta uttered then took a sip of her Martini.

"You may think this shit crazy, but it works for us." I watched Netta's body language and facial expressions as I told my story to get a feel for her. I was trying to see if I could flip her to join us.

"May I add that we don't keep secrets, and we're drama free. Our relationship is different, but we are happy," Breya added.

Netta drank a little more before she started to spill the beans about her man troubles. I motioned to the bartender to refill her glass while she talked. The more she drank, the more she spoke and revealed her frustrations with that whack ass nigga Chico. By the second drink, the three of us had shared laughs, danced, and got all worked up.

On the way from the head, I sat at the end of the bar and observed Breya and Antoinette interact with each other. Breya and I were undoubtedly into Netta. Right, then I imagined five different ways I wanted to fuck both of them and decided to buy another round of drinks. Breya sipped on her Grey Goose and cranberry juice while Antoinette enjoyed another Martini. The women were so fine, and their bodies screamed for attention. Netta's plump lips made my manhood hard as a rock. I could feel those lips wrapped around my shit. Her breasts sat up just right. I licked my lips because I wanted them in my mouth, but the timing was everything.

"How ya doing ladies? Are y'all almost ready to move this party back to the crib?" I had weed just in case she was a smoker who got super horny afterward.

"I'm feeling sooo good! This buzz is lovely," Netta confessed. Her glossy fuck me eyes twinkled.

"C'mon let's get out of here." I gestured towards the exit with my hand while both women walked in front of me.

The small talk between the women allowed me to watch their booties sway all the way to the parking lot.

The next morning I woke up satisfied I finally got a taste of Antoinette after all these years. She had to be the best threesome I'd had so far. I tugged on my dick while I laid next to Netta and them luscious titties.

"Morning."

"Hey, sexy mama," I said as she tried to hide her face behind her hand.

"Aye, how are you feeling? Girl, you were lit off of those Martinis and smoke. I had no idea you were that fun."

"Oh my goodness, what did I do? How bad did embarrass myself?"

I could see the embarrassment but quickly reassured her it was all good. "You were hot in every way last night. I didn't know smoking made you so generous with your body. We had some fun, but please don't beat yourself up."

"Shit, in my mind, sex is a part of life. There's nothing to be bashful about either. Everything we did was completely natural and will stay between us. Don't trip."

━━

It was my pleasure to drop Netta off at the bar to get her car because it gave us more time together. The ride was perfect because I needed to get to the barbershop anyway. Netta didn't talk much, but I was able to make her laugh a few times along the way.

Groomed up, I sat in the barber chair while Omar lined me up. In typical barbershop talk, we discussed sports, politics, and women. I gave his ass the rundown on the double scoops of pussy I'd been getting. Also in need of advice, I picked his brain on my next moves. I had fallen so hard for

Netta that she was all I thought about, wanted, and needed in my life.

Breya, on the other hand, was my life, my heart, and meant the world to me. We had a bond that no one would never understand. Inviting Netta in the picture had the potential to cause chaos down the line. Until that day came, I kept doing me, and the ladies enjoyed our lifestyle. We worked hard during the week and got down and dirty on the weekends.

CHAPTER 13

CHICO HAWKINS

I WAITED for Netta to bring her ass home; she was missing in action. She left me a note that stated she was with an old friend from high school. I figured she was trying to get back at me for fucking Keisha. It was after midnight night as I waited for her, so I watched *Ride Along 2* on HBO with a blunt in hand. Kevin Hart was a funny little muthafucka. My laughter filled the living room along with the smell of blueberry kush. When the movie ended, Netta still hadn't made it in. I called her ass so many times that it pissed me off each time. I rolled another blunt and played another movie.

Unaware I had fallen asleep, the sounds of footsteps woke me up. The morning sun shone brightly through the living room windows. Slowly, I sat up from the couch and rubbed my eyes as I heard Netta.

"Welcome home. I'm glad you finally made it. I was about to come looking for yo' ass." I said, facing her way.

"Chico, don't start with me. I went out and got drunk and smoked with friends. I deserve to have fun right. Shit, you out here doing what you want!" she shouted at me.

"Netta, you're always accusing me of doing something with a bitch. Stop that shit, man."

"I have text messages that say something different, *Mr. Sweet Dick*. That bitch gave you a nickname, yeah I know it all. The look on your face is the expression that I was waiting for, and you just confirmed what I knew. You busted, baby," she said and gave me an evil grin.

Wow, busted like a muthafucka I could not deny it. I always knew she was good at finding out shit. Keisha kept sending texts and apparently Netta saw them. There was no way out of this one, and from her looks, she was super pissed. Let me prepare for the worse of this situation. I collected my thoughts as I sat there looking stupid. What she said next fucked my head all the way up and made my chest hurt.

"Now that your secret is out, I will confess my own. I'm sure you won't like it. I was out with a high school friend and got drunk and high. Your recent messages and infidelity with Keisha pushed me to do something bad. I had a threesome and actually liked it. I liked it so much that I've decided to do it again and again."

I stood, mouth open, speechless. I couldn't believe she flat out told me that shit. The truth hurt, and I admit I had it coming. "What you mean a threesome? Who the fuck is this old friend?"

"I'm not telling you names, but it was a guy and girl. And I liked everything we did. I feel so free now that I got that off my chest. Karma is truly a bitch ain't it," she boasted and walked off.

Then she turned around and added, "By the way, it's over loser!"

"Oh hell naw, you got me fucked up, girl. You know

what. Let me get some shit so that I can get the fuck out of here. I can't afford to catch a case fucking around with you."

I went to the bedroom and grabbed a bunch of shit and threw it in a bag then stormed out. My name was on the lease, so moving out wasn't an option. That house was just as much mine too. But to avoid confrontation, I spent a night at my guy Bishop's house and a night at the hotel.

When I went back home, Netta went about her daily routine and treated a nigga like a roommate. No communication, meal prep, or acknowledgment, nothing but a cold shoulder. Within a week, shorty got mad disrespectful talking to that nigga on the phone in front of me. In the kitchen, by the sink, I had just rinsed off a few chicken breasts. Just as I sliced and seasoned them, Netta walked in with the phone pressed to her ear. That shit didn't bother me at first until she started giggling, and I saw her blushing like a high school girl. In an effort not to react, my focus remained on the food until I heard her make plans to meet up with ole boy. That last straw made me turn around to face the woman who had pushed the wrong button.

"Netta, you not gonna keep disrespecting. Go talk to the bitch ass nigga somewhere else in the house. I'm not trying to hear y'all shit."

"Umm, last time I checked this my house too, so I can talk on the phone in any room I fucking please. You just salty another nigga took an interest in me while you were fucking that bitch."

"Like I said take that shit somewhere else before I—" she cut me off and walked closer to me with the phone still in her hand.

"Before you what? You're not gonna do shit but finish cooking your meal and stay out my business. Now that the shoe is on the other foot, you all in your feelings. Boo hoo nigga, get over it." Off the phone, she stood closer.

"Bih, I'm never in my feelings remember that shit." I had just told a bald-faced lie, a nigga was salty how shit went down, leading them to the point of no return.

In the process of placing my cut-up chicken in the pan of hot oil, the sounds of banging alerted us. Not expecting company, I turned the eye off and removed the skillet before heading towards the front room.

"Who the fuck is banging on the door like that?" I gripped the handle snatched it open to find a nigga muggin' the shit out of me. Confused as fuck, I turned to Netta who stood in the shadows watching with a somewhat smirk on her face. I wanted to choke the hell out of her, but touching a woman was nothing a real man did.

"Nigga you bold as hell to show up on my steps like this."

"Aye Antoinette, you good?" That nigga had the nerve to ignore me as if I didn't ask him a question.

"Bruh, everything good here, take yo ass back where you came from. I should fuck you up for coming here but I'mma let you slide."

"Whatever, nigga. Aye Netta, as long as you good I'll leave, but this clown doesn't know who he's talking to."

He didn't scare me not one bit, but his words pissed me off. I walked off because I loved my freedom too much. To avoid them both, I went to the room and packed a bag. When angry, I preferred to be by myself because it was best for everyone's sake. I tended to say hurtful shit now and sometimes regretted it. Never so pissed I stormed out the house and jumped in my ride and sped off.

———

I checked into a hotel and paid a few days to get my shit together. I was still stunned that Netta revealed the shit to me about liking women and then broke up with me. I dived into the king-sized bed and lay back with my arms folded behind my head. It was time for me to think about the recent shit that happened and make changes. As I lay in silence, my mind wandered, and I thought about the last twenty-four hours and how I fucked up. Those few days at the hotel turned into a more extended stay to ensure my safety from Netta.

It was hard to believe Netta messed around with a woman and broke up with me. She did to me what I did to her, and it wasn't a good feeling. I guess that's what I get for sleeping around. My feelings and ego were crushed that she left me for another nigga and chick. I never knew her to be into girls, guess I really didn't know her at all. To ease the pain, liquor and Keisha's pussy were my drugs of choice.

I texted her my location, and without much convincing, she agreed to visit. A half an hour later, she hit me just as she hit the corner. I snatched the room key off the stand and headed for the elevator. On the ride down, I stopped at the front desk for towels. I hit the bar in need of several shots of Patrón until Keisha arrived.

"It can't be that bad!" a female voice exclaimed.

With a wide grin and slight turn of the body, there Keisha stood with her titties wooshed up. They practically jumped out from her shirt, making my mouth water from the thought of sucking them.

"If only you knew the half of it, baby girl. It doesn't matter anyway. Come sit for a minute and join me." I flagged the bartender our way for a few more before the party moved upstairs.

"I'll have two shots of whatever he's drinking and a Patrón and lemonade," she requested with confidence.

"Is there ever a time when you don't look appetizing? It's very hard to look and not touch."

"Don't trip. After these drinks, you can touch every inch of my body," she teased just as the shot glasses were placed in front of her. She threw them back one after another, squeezing her eyes shut from the taste.

"Oh yeah, we about to have some fun, girl!" It didn't take her long to finish up before I took her to the room.

While Keisha slept, I observed her naked body amazed at how she worked it while we fucked. Almost obsessed, I yawned and craved her in an unhealthy way. Laid beside each other, I played with her nipples using the palm of my hand. That same hand slid down between her legs just to rub her kat. The light stubbles of hair against my fingers got my aroused all over again. My index finger explored her slippery lips before slowly entering inside. Warm like apple pie, her pussy had magical powers. Addicted, I wanted more and more of her.

After my solo freak session, I took a quick shower and dressed only to find her still sleep. I went back down for another drink and to think about my future. Time had finally come for me to get my shit together.

Around ten at night, I had a good buzz going and hoped Keisha was ready for another go around. Sex had been the only thing on my mind since Netta and I separated. In route to 421, some random ass nigga bumped into me, so of course, I had a few words for him. Before I knew it, that nigga snatched me up and punched the shit out of me. The shit happened so fast that my reaction time was delayed, and I ended up in a fucked up situation.

When I came to and looked around the room, all I saw was plastic and shit. My heart began to beat through my shirt. Never did it occur to me that my life had become in grave danger. Unsure who the fuck he was all types of shit rumbled through my head as I tried to think of an escape plan. At first, I thought Netta's new male friend sent him, but when the name Erika left his lips, a chill flowed through my body. At that moment, I knew nothing good would come from the situation. A picture collage of life's moments flashed through my head, including the recent sexual activities. I smiled and took my last breath and thought of Keisha.

CHAPTER 14

ANTOINETTE NIXON

WHEN MONEY APPEARED on the other side of the door it dawned on me he heard Chico and I arguing. Never did it occur to me that he would pop up at my house. The strange thing about the whole situation was that I never told Money where I lived. Either way, I'd never had a man come to my rescue the way he did. Chico's facial expression served as a priceless moment, appalled that a nigga showed up to our door out of concern for my safety. I stood there and stared at the two of them have a face-off.

"Nigga, you got some fucking nerves showing up at my shit. Are you her new man now?"

"As a matter of fact, I am since you can't treat a lady right. I'll take over. And another thing, watch how you talk to her, homie. That's how you get fucked up."

"Okay, calm down both of y'all!" I shouted. In between the men, Money turned around to walk away as I followed behind him.

"Wow! That went left real fast. I'm sorry. I didn't mean to get you involved in my mess."

"No need to apologize, ma. I don't like that nigga talking disrespectfully to you."

"It's basically over between us anyway. I'm not happy, so I need to move around. He cheats and then has the nerve to get pissed at me."

"You don't need that shit. He's not a real man, and definitely not the one. Shit, you already know how I feel!" he exclaimed.

We talked and walked as we made it close to his parked car. He gave me peace and made me smile. Money made me feel a way Chico couldn't, which prompted me to think carefully on how to proceed with him.

"To be honest, Breya's digging you too, but that's another topic for another time. I gotta go do a few things. You gonna be alright?"

Still taken aback from his statement about his girl liking me, I barely paid attention to what he said afterward. "Huh? What?"

"You gonna be alright here with that punk ass nigga around? Otherwise, you can pack a bag and come to our place."

"I should be good here. He not that stupid, I'll kill him before he lay hands on me. This situation has definitely opened my eye that's for sure. Thanks again for coming to my see me."

Money got inside his vehicle, and when he drove away, I took a deep breath and walked back to the house. From that day on, I went about my daily business until I got the call about moving into my new spot.

At some point and time, a woman gets tired of waiting for a nigga to get some sense and act right. I was fed up with Chico and his shit, so it was best I removed myself from the situation. It was the same shit different day with his ass, and to add insult to injury, it was lie after lie right in front of my face. Chico had a spot in my heart, but his games were for children. Even though Money was cool, he had a girlfriend so exploring that option wasn't gonna happen.

In the mirror, I looked at myself and decided enough was enough. Chico could kiss my ass because it was over. At some point and time, a woman got tired of waiting for a nigga to change. Single, smart, and still young, I had the world readily available. Instead of soaking in the change, I embraced it as an opportunity. From the second I stepped out the house for good a feeling of freedom came over me. Able to find a lovely two-bedroom house, it was a new beginning for my dreams and me. I changed my mindset and focused on my education by taking a few classes at MATC.

⸺

When I moved into a two-bedroom, the reality hit me that I was on a new journey. The first few nights were cool, and it was peaceful, but I missed the random sex with Chico. Lying under the covers dressed in a pair of panties and tank top, I grew horny. My memories of Breya and Money sucking my breasts intensified the urge. I masturbated, in order to keep from hooking up with a lame person I'd regret. Something had to give. It was time to live, venture out, and make new friends in the process.

Ironically, Money sent me a message to meet up with him and Breya for a bite to eat. We met at the same place the night we hooked up they had good food. When I arrived, the two of them sat together sipping a beverage scanning the menu. Somewhat jealous of their relationship, the smile on my face hid my true feelings.

"Hey y'all, I hope I'm not late," I said, taking a seat across from them.

"Nope, you're on time actually. Here you can look at my menu," Breya insisted, as she slid it to me and kept talking. "Money told me about your guy Chico, and I've been thinking about something. Please don't take this the wrong way but Money told me about his interest in you."

Breya's lips moved, and all I could think about was how weird it was to be around her wearing clothes. Her words went through one ear and out the other as my smile never left my face. That is until I heard her ask me if I wanted to join their team.

"Join your team as in what?" I asked as I felt my forehead wrinkle, followed by a frown of confusion.

"I figured since we had so much fun that night and you're not with Chico, the three of us could hook up. You don't have to move in with us or accept the offer. It just seems so right."

Unsure how to respond, I waved a hand in the air for the attention of our server. A short squeaky-voiced woman attended to us and our orders. Although mid-day, I ordered an alcoholic beverage immediately to digest their proposition. They were bold, open, and showed no shame in the game.

"Like Breya was saying, we figured it would be a win-win type of situation for us all. Antoinette, please consider it, that's all we ask of you, no pressure."

"In a strange way the offer is tempting, the best of both worlds was worth exploring. Let me sleep on it. I'll need some time because that type of arrangement could cause conflict."

"That is the beauty of you having your own place, come and go as you please. Spend a few nights a month, or however, we agree." Breya stopped talking until the server sat all of our plates on the table and walked away.

"As the man, it has been my fantasy to live a polygamy lifestyle, and each of you has made it a reality. Beyond sex, I legit love you women. Y'all both got a certain way of life."

Glad to have food in front of me, it was my excuse not to speak much. I thought about how nice it would be to have access to dick at all times. The thought of having my pussy ate by a dude and a chick was definitely something to think about. Between bites full of pasta, I slid in a few laughs and head nods. It would settle my horny nights, but the complications made me hesitant.

"Aye Antoinette, have you ever seen the *Fifty Shades* movies? Maybe a movie night with pizza, wine, and smoke will help relax you."

I swallowed before speaking. "I bought the first book but never finished it, nor have I seen the movies. Every time I turn to HBO, the movie is in the middle or almost over."

"Well, we have all of the movies. It will be fun. How about this Saturday once I get home from work?"

"Okay. I'll swing by after I stop home from class." Breya's convincing charm led me to answer without thinking.

The second I accepted the offer my panties got wet from the mere thought of what might happen. Low key I began to question my sexuality because of how aroused I became from a woman. Either way, being single gave me the option to explore and live my life.

I decided to grab the bill as a kind gesture just to show them the type of person they were dealing with. I removed my Visa debit card and slid it into the black holder for the server to grab.

"Oh, you didn't have to do that," Breya's said just as the waitress quickly walked past and grabbed the black holder.

"It's all good! I believe that doing small things like this brings good karma. Besides you know the motto, you have to give to receive."

"Here you go. Have a good one and thank you for stopping by," the waitress said and flashed a smile before moving on to her other customers.

The three of us got up from the table and strolled out of the restaurant doors together. Outside Money moved in for a hug, so when I extended my arms to embrace him, he lined his body with mine. When he lightly squeezed me, I also felt him push his manhood against me.

"Oh." I laughed and jumped. Breya then moved in for a hug as well, which was short and sweet.

"Alright, I'll talk to y'all in a few days. I got a lot of reading to do for class next week. Have a good evening."

Money said, "Yeah, alright, but don't be a stranger."

"I won't! See ya." I turned and walked away, still shocked as I climbed inside the car and drove off.

After the meal with Money and Breya, I fell back for a week to focus on my studies. Shit, I also needed time to think about how to proceed if I joined their relationship. In the library at a table alone on the second floor, I must of read the same sentence three times. The conversation about polygamy had been tripping me out because it never crossed my mind. My interest in the topic became so intriguing that I decided to pack up and move to a computer. I typed "polyamorous relationships" in the search engine and found a few articles and videos worth exploring.

Before departing the library, I made sure to clear my browsing history then logged out. Safely home food, shower, and videos kept me occupied the rest of the night. After watching three videos, my whole perspective changed on the topic. Although the sex part alone intrigued me, the openness that Money and Breya shared made me think. So intrigued, I even sent Money a text.

Me: *Aye, I've been thinking. We need to chat privately to discuss something. When can you come over?*

Watching some of those videos got me a little bothered between the legs. So much so I put the phone down and went to grab a small bottle of Pink Moscato from the kitchen counter. By the time my ass sat down to grab the phone, a message had come through.

Money: *Everything good??? My shift is over in thirty. Let me know if you want me to drop by on the way home.*

Me: *Oh, everything is cool. I just need to... Yeah, if it's not a bother could you please come on over!*

While waiting for him to reply, I cracked open the first bottle and took a few gulps. Instead of doing homework, my mind focused on sex and my willingness to try something new with Money and Breya. I continued to watch videos and sipped until the phone beeped, causing me to get excited.

Money: *On the way to your spot. Need anything?*

Me: *Your dick!*

Money: *Damn! Just like that little nasty. Your wish is my command.*

Me: *I'll be waiting.*

Money had turned me into a curious little freak, and I couldn't believe my recent behavior. I automatically jumped up to make sure my bedroom and bathroom were clean then changed out of my pajama bottoms into a pair of black boxer shorts. They were the cute kind that displayed my perfect shape. Already showered, I waited for my company. A quick twirl in the body mirror, Money's knock at the door caused me to jump. All smiles and a semi-buzz, I headed in the direction of the door and twisted the knob to open it.

"Umm... Netta why you have to do this to me? Baby, you look scrumptious," he confessed.

When he licked his lips, I snatched him inside, closed the door, and kissed him as I'd never done before. He started to strip out of his jacket, followed by his shirt and reach around to grab my ass.

"Aye baby I need to hop in the shower right quick. I probably smell like sausage."

"Sausage is all I want right now," I joked. "Go ahead and do what you gotta do. I'll be in bed waiting for you."

"Good shit. Oh, I got this too if you want a few hits," he handed me half a blunt from his pocket.

He went to the bathroom to clean up while I went to my room to light a few medium candles from Bath and Body Works. Minutes later, the fragrance of lavender and vanilla filled the room. On the bed, I patiently waited for Money to join me. He then appeared before me with the blue bath towel wrapped around his waist.

"Bring your sexy ass to me right now," I demanded ready to feel his penetration.

"Who are you, and where is Netta? Tonight I see that other side of you again. I love it too," he admitted then dropped his towel.

"YES! I've missed y'all," I said, gripping my hand around his dick and teased it with the tip of my tongue.

The scent from his Axe body washed turned me on

even more. He slid in the bed with me and fired up the blunt. The feeling of having a body next to me felt natural, not to mention a dream come true.

"Aye earlier you said you wanted to talk about something. What about?"

"I was thinking about our conversation last week about joining the team. I did some research and just tried to get a better understanding of it all. It's still stuff that puzzles me, but I want to do this."

He passed the blunt to me and exhaled as he rubbed my inner thigh then moved towards my pussy. In ecstasy from a combination of the weed and his touch, I suddenly felt the urge to act on my thoughts. I moved in position and took his dick in my mouth, wrapping my lips around it. Blow jobs were something I liked to do because it turned me on too. Once I licked and sucked him like a sucker to his peak, I stopped and looked him in the eye.

"I want you to fuck me so good that I won't be able to walk tomorrow. My body needs attention from you right now. Give it to me, baby!"

"You've been so reckless tonight! I love that mouth of yours, Netta baby. Come ride this dick now."

"Grab a Magnum from the drawer," I ordered while doing a cat crawl towards him.

He slid the condom on and carefully eased on his stiff beef stick inch by inch until he was all the way inside. After a few strokes being on top didn't satisfy me, so we switched positions. Bent over on my knees, Money entered me from the back and grabbed my titties. I closed my eyes and let my body enjoy the pleasures of each hard thrust.

Money had sex appeal and bomb dick that I had grown attached to, and I needed his loving. The more he fucked me; it became clear why Keisha wouldn't leave Chico alone, good dick.

"Ahh!" I moaned feeling like a different woman. "Fuck me, baby just like that! Oh, my goodness."

"Netta this pussy got me hooked. This can't be real. Shiiit! I'm about to come."

"Me too," I shouted.

"FUUUCK!"

The two of us grunted and breathed heavily as he pulled out of me and slapped me on the ass. He kissed my lips, and when he turned to head to the bathroom, I returned the favor and popped him on his ass.

"Look at them little cheeks," I joked.

He came out of the bathroom just in time because my bladder almost failed me. By the time I cleaned up and exited the bathroom, Money had been fully dressed with his phone in hand.

"Aye, tonight made me realize I got a life to live. Thank you for fucking some sense into me. Tell Breya that I'm down."

"Already did. She just texted me wondering when I'm coming home."

"Y'all good?"

"Yeah. At first, she said she felt salty, but she alright now."

"So I guess we'll hook up soon to discuss the stipulations of our agreement? I have lots of questions for you two."

"I'm sure you do. The main rule is to never step outside of our relationship, no matter what. We don't fuck outside the group unless there is a unanimous vote. We can do another lunch or dinner and discuss shit in detail. I gotta get up out of here. A nigga is tired."

"Why don't you just sleep here? I promise not to take

advantage of you while you sleep. It makes more sense than getting out here this late."

"Fuck it. I'll let Breya know, so she doesn't flip out on my ass."

Still naked and comfortable, I watched him slip his shoes back off and walked into the kitchen. He came back with two bottles of water and a bowl of green grapes. We Netflix and chilled for a few more hours until we passed out. Drifting off to sleep in his arms made me feel wanted and loved. I didn't fully know what the hell I had gotten into, but I had been ready to take a risk.

CHAPTER 15

KENTRELL "MONEY" GIPSON

THAT THREESOME WITH Netta and my girl was all I could think about lately, so much so that it made Breya look at me sideways. Wrong on so many levels, I couldn't help reliving the feelings from the adventurous night. That was my first time touching and tasting my high school crush. Never in a million years did I imagine my wish would come true. Don't get me wrong. I really did love my girlfriend, but Antoinette was the one who got away. She used to hurt all the hearts of the boys at school when she turned them down.

The talks on the phone turned into house visits where the two of us spent half the time just having sex. The other half, we talked about our goals and how to step our game up. She encouraged me to do what truly made me happy above anything else. Netta was truly a beautiful soul, and it wrecked my brain how the hell Chico fucked things up with her. Either way, it worked out because he was out of the picture, and I got the girl.

The morning I left Netta's spot I noticed a note stuck under the windshield wipers. I approached with caution turning my head to look around. The minute I retch for the piece a paper, I heard someone walk up behind me. A man's voice stopped me from turning around.

"I won't hurt you, but I'll shoot you without blinking." The man stated as he pressed the barrel of a gun at my head.

"I don't want any fucking trouble. If Chico punk ass sent you, —" he cut me off from speaking.

"No one sent me. That nigga is on my list. Let's take a quick ride around the block," he demanded.

I let out a sigh of relief when I felt the gun being removed from my head. Slowly I proceeded to the driver's side, that's when my eyes caught a glimpse of him. He dressed in all in black, professional, a man who meant business. We climbed inside my ride as the gun remained pointed in my direction.

"Let me ask you, how did you know I'd be here?" I took a chance to question as I started the engine.

"I've been watching you and your girl. I thought she was Chico's chick?"

"What?" I jerked my head back with a frowned face confused why that nigga had been following me.

"Chico's days are numbered. What do you know about him?"

"I don't know shit. He a loser ass dude who was cheating on his girl. Other than that I can't tell you shit," I spat.

"Hmm," he sat in the passenger idle.

"Aye, we don't have shit to do with him nor do we care about what happens to him. In my honest opinion, he deserves the karma that comes his way. Now can we forget this shit happened?"

"Word. Drop me at my car and go about your business. I

don't know you and you don't know me," the mysterious man confirmed.

I had just made a right turn at the lights headed back towards Netta's place. The entire time all I could do was wonder who he was and what Chico did. Then again, it didn't surprise me that he had a target on his back. From the first time I laid eyes on him, I knew his ass was no good. When I pulled up in front of Netta's he proceeded to exit the car, but before he did he said one last thing that had me bugging out.

"Remember I can find you and anyone you love. Oh, you a playa for having two chicks at the same time. Just make sure that shit don't backfire on you. Holla black nigga," he warned.

"Thanks for the reminder," I replied. I watched him hop in his ride and pull off before I got out. Afterward, I rushed to tell Netta what had just happened.

⊏⊐

A week later, I couldn't stop thinking about what that nigga told me about having two chicks. It made me think about my pops and the shit I saw as a child. Growing up, my dad had a different chick every day of the week, and for a long time, I thought that shit was dope. That fool was a rolling stone and laid his hat in multiple homes. He did whatever he wanted whenever because he dared anyone to tell him different. Sadly, laying his hat among other things cost him his life at age forty.

Apparently one of the women he'd messed with had a husband who got an early release from prison. In less than forty-four hours that nigga killed both my dad and the chick for her infidelity. He went right back to lock up without getting a chance to enjoy freedom. A few weeks after the funeral, my mother eventually broke down, and at that moment, I realized the power of a woman. My mother eventually cracked up when another woman claimed to be pregnant. Shit was never the same moving forward, so much so that she stopped caring what I did.

Into adulthood, I picked up at least one bad habit from my dad— loving more than one woman. Unlike the old man, I didn't mess with married women, nor did I lie about my sexual preferences in a relationship. My interest in polyamory went exactly from an interest to straight practice. Hence how Breya and I met, but what we shared turned into a full-blown relationship. She too shared an interest in women, and that shit stunned me yet turned me on at the same time. Breya, the sexual explorer, even came up with the idea to have a threesome every other month. As time passed the bond and love we shared grew no matter how many threesomes.

Unlike things on the home front, the job scene had been a little confrontational. It was promotion time, not to mention a few open positions. A few colleagues displayed their jealous trait by backstabbing each other and ass kissing to the boss. Although I needed the raise, it wasn't my style to sell myself short. I prided myself on getting shit on my terms, not kissing ass from anybody.

I'd been working for Klement's Sausage Co. close to four years in multiple roles. As the current QA Technician, it was time to move up to the production supervisor since I'd been basically doing both jobs. During my spare time, I spent a few hours searching for a new job. It was my backup plan just in case I had to fuck somebody up or got fired. Lately, a few of the employees had lost their fucking mind making slick comments and whatnot. They just didn't know the old me would've fucked them up. I had too much to lose. Therefore, my actions remained professional.

Before going legit, I made a living hustling like my cousin who pushed pills, weed, and anything else that made a profit. The hustle lasted long enough for me to save about $4500 before shit got dismantled. My cousin went to jail, while my lucky ass made a clean escape without ruining my record. Only fifteen years old at the time, I thought doing grown folks shit made me tough. Displaying the typical behavior of a teenager, I learned how to act accordingly once my mother made a promise to let me rot in jail. Eventually, I got my act together by the time I turned eighteen.

CHAPTER 16

ERIKA CAIN

TYREE and I were better acquainted and became cool as fuck. We would hit each other line to hang, blow, and watch movies. Sex didn't enter the equation until months later, but the tension between us was apparent. My hormones went haywire. I took enough cold showers and burned out my vibrator that I needed the real thang. Tyree was like a sweet potato pie that I could no longer resist. Almost seven months of learning to open up and enjoy the company of a man, together we helped each other face our fears. Trust and loyalty were the two things we lived by, our code of life.

I made a quick run to CITGO first then to Pick N' Save for snacks and a small container of sour cream for the taco salad. My forgetful ass always left the store missing an item the first time around. While I drove from the store back to the condo, my phone rang, but I couldn't answer. Not bothering to check it, I moved from the car inside to the kitchen area. The meat was already cooked and covered along with all condiments included. I took a break to use my thumb unlocked my iPhone.

"Damn, I missed Tyree call!" I shouted aloud. "Siri, call Tyree," I instructed.

"What's da word, E Baby? A nigga's back for a week, and I got a new batch of cookies. What it do?"

"Hey T, shit I'm always down to try something new. Aye, I just browned some ground beef and got shit for nachos. I got food, and you got the smoke. We need to link up right now."

"Hell yeah, I'm on my way," he acknowledged.

"Cool. See you when you arrive," I replied before we disconnected.

I flew through the place making sure that shit was straight. I couldn't have Tyree thinking that I kept a dirty home. I took the quickest shower ever and rubbed down with lotion. The sound of the buzzer tempted me to grab the first thing I could. On the way down the stairs, I slipped on a V-Neck wrap around dress, pulling it down to cover myself. With no bra or panties on my thot, voice egged me on to be flirty. With a deep breath, a smile graced my face as I opened the door.

"Right on time, come on in."

He stood still for a second as his gaze cruised over my figure. The navy blue V-neck dress was knee length but hugged my apple bottom shape. He licked his lips and slowly strolled inside while I closed and locked the door behind him.

"I'm sorry for my language, but I'd rather have you for dinner, no offense to the nachos."

"Dude, you're a character," I laughed it off. Shit, I really wanted him to take me up the stairs to have his way with me.

"I'm just honest, that's all. I'm too grown not to speak

my mind. Besides you already knew the response that I would give you wearing that sexy ass shit. It's cute."

"Thanks. Umm, feel free to wash your hands and fix a plate.

Tyree did just that as I blushed until he looked my way. I put my cool face on. Changing the topic, I washed my hands, opened the bag of cheese Doritos, and piled them on a plate followed by ground beef. I loved to load on lettuce, diced tomatoes, with a sprinkle of jalapeno peppers and hot melted cheese. I saved the sour cream and mild Ortega sauce for last. Tyree was practically drooling at the presentation of my plate.

"Yo', that shit is hooked! I'm about to do mine the same way, minus the tomatoes."

"Go for what you know," I encouraged and sat in the high back black chair at the counter across from him.

The image of a man in my kitchen fixing a plate was like an eclipse, a rare occasion. It was something to definitely get accustomed to, but shit had to work out first. Military men tended to snap out from time to time.

"Aye before you sit, may I please get lemonade from the refrigerator? Thanks."

Together we sat and enjoyed a quick, simple meal over, pleasant conversation and laughs. Like longtime friends, our body language became normal towards each other. Not ashamed to smash food in front of him, I cleaned my plate. We got to talking about movies, music, in addition to real life shit as I cleaned up the kitchen. From there, we moved a few steps over to the living room area for a movie. Tyree's eyes danced at the sight of my ass in motion.

"Hey Cortana, turn on!" I shouted in front of the 45-inch flat screen and Xbox One. I had my devices set on voice command because the remote always ended up lost or ended upstairs.

"You're such a different type of chick. I swear I wanna marry yo' ass woman. Aye, can we blow one? I brought you some special to try. It's called Strawberry Satori. I promise you will fall in love with the smell and taste."

"Hell yeah, I'm down. Hold up, let me get you my kit so that you don't make a mess on my floor."

I got up and went upstairs to retrieve the lockbox where I kept all of my weed paraphernalia. While up there, I slipped on a pair of black bikini cut panties and returned downstairs. "While you do that I'll find something on Amazon Prime Video. How about *American Gangster* with my boy Denzel Washington?"

"That will work for me, sweet cheeks!"

"I beg your pardon?"

"You got some sweet cheeks! When you got up to run upstairs, you flashed me a little bit. Nothing but yellow meat in my face."

"Boy, you play too much! My bad though. I didn't feel like putting on panties. I wanted to let my girl breath."

I got up one more time to close the blinds on all of the windows then finally sat next to him. On the soft, cozy plush gray loveseat, I commanded Cortana to play the movie. Tyree lit the blunt, and immediately, the smell was to die for, but when I inhaled it, umm. The taste was light, fruity, and smooth.

"How you like it? That shit fire?"

"First time having it, yes, I love it! You need to break me off a little before you leave."

"I'll get you some for your stash."

Once the blunt vanished, we sat in stuck mode high as a kite until the part of the movie when Denzel snapped about the Alpaca carpet. One of the funniest parts of the movie, Tyree and I caught the giggles and shit. With a real high going, my sensual need for touch kicked in as I cut my eyes in his direction. It was so many freaky things I wanted to do with him, but I tried to figure out the easiest way to approach the situation.

"Do you mind if I stretch my legs across yours? It feels like a cramp is forming," I asked to give him a subtle hint.

"Shit, it took you long enough to ask. I've been waiting to rub on those hams. Who knows you might let me rub something else."

"Okay, from the little comments you been making all evening, it's clear you feel how I do. I'm ready to take our friendship to the next level, but don't want shit to get weird."

"I don't catch feelings, but let's keep it real for a minute. You know a little about me but not everything. On some real shit, you are the first woman to entice me in more than the sexual manner. However, to answer your question, I've been ready to tear that ass up. I want to fuck the shit out of you."

"Say no more, baby! That smoke got me horny right now, and trust, I'm long overdue for some action. Tonight you get a pass to the second floor for some show and tell time."

"Let's move around then. Show me the way to the special palace." He licked his lips followed with an eye wink, made a bitch wet instantly.

I stood up only to feel him slap me on the ass. I gave him "fuck me eyes" while turning the television off. He took the cue and followed behind me up the stairs. With each step, I got excited about the unknown with him like what size was the dick and how was his tongue game. It was still up in the air if he was worthy of spending the night.

"Well, this is my palace. I love my room, but the bathroom is hot. Go peep at it."

"This bathroom is the truth! The Jacuzzi tub is exactly what I need from all the traveling."

"And you are what I need right now. Care for some music?" R-Kelly nasty ass was the inspiration needed.

Tyree began to pull off his shirt and wife beater, exposing nothing but abs and chest. His caramel skin was like the creamy filling in a candy bar. He was my dessert, and I couldn't get enough of him. With a chiseled body, the tattoos plastered on his upper body made his ass finer than any man I've come across. My mama's rules went out the window within a matter of weeks.

Tyree walked towards me and proceeded to undress me. Without hesitancy, I let the feelings take over my body. In ecstasy, every touch enhanced from the weed, stimulation was at an all-time high. On the bed, I inventoried his dick region, ready to see him unleash the monster. Tuh, when those boxers came off, I cocked a brow in surprise. It should be a law for a man to carry around a weapon so thick and long. It was clear why some men walked a certain way, carrying a dick as Tyree owned would make any man limp.

"Oh my, that shit is..." I couldn't even finish my sentence from being so hypnotized by his manhood. With the lights dim, the stroll lights added to the mode.

"Fucking a nigga like me is dangerous, ain't no going back once I slide inside."

"Same here, this pussy is like gold that I protect by any means necessary. Once you enter the silk purse, I have the right to fuck you up whenever I feel obligated. We got a deal?"

"Yo crazy ass is the perfect woman I've been searching for all this time!" I held his gaze without blinking while I laid back invitingly.

"Let me stroke that silk purse the way you deserve, baby!"

Aroused soon as his hands rubbed up to my legs to the inner thighs, my flower blossomed open. First, he teased me with a few rubs, and then his middle finger slipped inside me at medium speed. His finger slid in and out and explored the lips. The pleasure was the only thing I felt as a relaxed orgasm released inside of me.

Before I knew it, the warmth of his tongue was lapping around my shit, giving me what he promised. It was something about getting good ass head from a nigga who does it right with no instructions needed. On my back swarming like a worm, I held a fist full of the sheets in both hands. His eating game was a ten out of ten if I had to rate it. He reminded me the dick was yet to come as he rubbed the head of his snake against my lips.

"Aye, nigga don't split my shit with that monster ass pipe you touting. I do value the ability to walk. Be gentle, or I will be forced to shoot yo ass in payback."

"Be quiet and take this dick, girl." I felt a slight pinch as his pole slowly entered inch by inch.

"Ooh... Yeah. That is the spot, YES!"

We started nice and slow. The intimate phase then ended up speeding things up. It got so rough that I could feel his shit hit my stomach a few times. Tyree gave long dicking a new meaning. He touched all parts of my insides. At the climax phase "Marry the Pussy" played just as Tyree was about to get his nut off.

"Damn Kellz, I feel you nigga, this p-u-s-s-y is the

bomb.com!" From the rhythm and sounds, I knew he was close to letting go.

An hour later, we relieved the tension and juices that were bottled inside. We took turns washing up before sleep took over and knocked us both out.

━━━

Waking up next to Tyree the next morning shocked me, but then a smile appeared. *"The power of the pussy will get you any and everything you desire sweetheart,"* my mother words echoed in my head as I observed him. With the right hand, I leaned over and grabbed his meat. I had to examine it again. With the sunlight assisting, I had a clear visual. His shit had to be at least seven or eight inches.

"Damn," I said out loud before I knew it.

"Morning, miss freaky! You want some more, huh?"

"I didn't know you were awake. My bad. Actually, I was just admiring your tool and how you used it last night."

"That was just the beginning. I got something different each time, baby! After I take a leak, can we get in the tub together?"

Hell-bent on getting his ass in the tub, I agreed. The two of us climbed out of bed and headed for the bathroom. He went straight to the toilet while I ran water. Already naked, we immersed our bodies in the warm bubbles.

"So what's on your agenda for the day if you don't mind me asking?"

"I gotta make a few moves around the city, then smoking and resting. I have a job in Chicago coming up. Thank you for treating a nigga like a king, feeding me and shit."

"When I'm cool with a person, I look out and ride for

them. Our friendship is special because we share an under-standing and we fucking. That's an automatic relationship because I don't fuck random niggas."

"That's something we need to chat about now. I've never been this close to a woman in my life. I don't know what love is or how it feels, but when we together feelings come alive."

"Dido. I'll confess the same thing, but I know the feeling all too well, and not all men can handle it. I never told anyone this not even Keisha or my mom, but a college boyfriend tried to kill me. Our meaning of love was very different, and he refused to understand I didn't love him the way he obsessed over me."

"Oh hell naw, that ain't cool. I'll find that nigga and cancel his life if you give me the word."

"NO!"

Damn, I talk too much. He did not need to know that part of my past. His ass got some evil inside of him that my ass never wants to see, I thought laid back as the bubbles massaged the lower part of my back.

"So back to your comment about us fucking and it meaning we're in a relationship. You need to know some shit about me then. When days go by, and you don't hear from me, please don't trip or think a nigga ignoring you. I'm working, that's all."

"What does your job entail?"

"I'm a reaper. I kill very bad people," he bluntly answered.

At a loss for words all I could do was stare at him in disbelief of the new found information. Rapidly blinking, I tried to process what he told me, still not able to speak. Instead, I wondered what the hell I had gotten myself into.

"You okay ma? I knew you weren't ready to hear my

truth. I just wanted to keep shit real, no secrets," Tyree admitted.

Damn this nigga probably crazy as shit. Why did I have to fuck him? I hope he not one of those crazy men from the Lifetime movies. On the other hand, I'm crazy too and we'd be two dead asses. Look at those sexy lips on him, I thought finally able to put together a sentence.

"I'll never sweat or press you. As long as I'm treated right and you don't lie to me, we good, baby."

"You got my word. Erika don't play with me, if we together, that's what it is. Don't be out here entertaining these niggas. Give me your word," he demanded.

"You the only nigga I plan to entertain."

Tyree had that type of authoritative voice the type to turn me on, especially when he called himself laying down the law. I stood up, titties right in his face, and climbed out of the tub. Showing my pearly whites, he followed suite snatching a towel to pat dry.

"You really want this D, huh. C'mon let me tap that ass." With a grin, he scooped me up with his strong arms. In the mood for hardcore fucking, he delivered again, resulting in three orgasms.

Not able to move right away afterward, he washed his piece and got dressed. A soft kiss on the forehead sealed the deal, Tyree and I had officially crossed that line. Relationships with men tended to be complicated when the sex was mind-blowing. As I escorted him to the door, wild thoughts filled my head.

The second he left, I ran my ass up the stairs, to call Keisha because I told her ass almost everything anyway. With him going away, it gave me time to think about moving forward. The voice of my mother nagged at me. I guess it was her way of sending a warning.

CHAPTER 17

TYREE LYONS

ERIKA MADE a nigga feel comfortable in her home. It was something I got used to whenever she invited me over. That's something I never did around anyone besides my broski Tristan. Her crib was nice for a single chick, clean and classy just like her. A woman with drive and intelligence turned me on even more than the physical attributes. A total package of the perfect woman, Erika was my new bae. During the drive back to the crib, that joint "G.O.A.T." by Eric Bellinger blasted through my speakers. It was definitely a theme song to describe how I felt. Women couldn't be trusted, but Erika proved different. I was still playing it carefully though she didn't know my occupation.

I grew closer with Erika to the point we could read each other's thoughts, facial expressions, and specific looks that didn't require the exchange of words. Each time I traveled away for a job, she confessed how much more she missed me. As a nigga who was tossed aside like trash, the feeling of being loved and cared for was foreign at first. It was a fuck buddy thing turned into a commitment to one person. I'll confess the sex was bomb as hell too.

The longer we were together, the easier it was to detect when Erika was mad, sad, happy, or in between. Her telltale signs always gave it away, even when she tried to lie. Her lips pouted when she was hungry, and the wrinkles in her forehead formed followed by slick comments. I loved her flirting ways when she got horny. She did two things, in particular, to let me know when she wanted it. Erika had a habit of dropping her towel right in front of me or she'd stare at me infatuated with those "fuck me" eyes. When it came to pleasing her in the bedroom, I gave her my best game each time.

Sex with her was magical, and I don't know if it was because I hadn't been with that many females, or she was just that good. Her yellow ass cheeks flopped up and down as she twerked my dick. Damn, she knew how to ride a nigga. It made me feel like I was in ecstasy. Her pussy was on fire, every time. Every angle I hit was hot. I swear that chick was the best I've ever had. She had a nigga crying aloud and shit. Everything about her pussy was good. Her mouth game was da off the chain, and she slobbed on my knob like a fudge bomb pop.

I loved it when she kissed my neck and nibble on my ear. The shit drove me crazy. Fun in the hot tub became a ritual at least three times a week, giving us the chance to play. Playtime with her was beyond exciting. It was something new I learned about her.

━━━

The more time that passed, I stepped up my game and made an official commitment to Erika. Tired of driving from my place to see her all the time, we agreed to share a place. This was a major deal for both of us, two single people sharing a space for the first time. It also brought out potential problems that most couples tended to have once the honeymoon stage faded. Both of us were strong minded and opinionated people.

Prime example, Erika had a bad habit of doing petty shit just to get a reaction out of me. The other problem was her smart-ass mouth, but that shit honestly turned me on. It was like she knew how far to go. So when I left the toilet seat up for the umpteenth time, she made sure I knew it. After several sarcastic remarks, I already knew what time it was, so I got up in a motion to leave for a few hours.

Before her ass could start cursing and nagging a nigga, I grabbed a duffle bag with some clothes and made my way to the door. As soon as I twisted the doorknob to exit, the sound of glass breaking stopped me. The shattered pieces flew past my face, damn near hitting me. Politely I pushed the door closed and dropped my bag.

"Oh hell no! You about to learn today. I'm not that nigga!" I spat, fed up with her bullshit.

When I turned around, she threw another glass jar in my direction, but I ducked it. My initial reaction caused me to grab her by the neck with my two hands. It took all of my power not to choke the life out of her ass.

"Why the fuck do you make me do this, huh?" I muttered through gritted teeth as I stood inches away from her face. With nostrils flaring, I had temporarily blacked out, but the smell of her cupcake lip gloss brought me back to reality.

"I never want to lay hands on yo' ass, but you're pushing me. What the fuck is your problem? I fucking hate you at times." I could see the anger in her eyes as they filled up with tears. When I released my hands from her neck, she coughed and caught her breath.

"Nigga, you are what's wrong with me. I'm tired of you and your bullshit. Ever since we moved in together, shit changed. The only thing on my mind is them dead presidents and yo' black ass. But guess what nigga, all that is about to change!" she shouted.

"Erika, do what you have to do because I don't need this shit. You know the type of shit I do so my head must remain clear from all distractions!" I yelled out.

"Hold the fuck up! We both made an agreement

"Yeah, but it doesn't really matter though. I will tell you this. That nigga's time is almost up and if you are with him then..."

"Then what? Oh, so you threaten me too. Nigga, get the fuck out of here. Do what you gotta do but remember this baby, I ain't never scared."

"I'm gone," I said and retrieved my bag and walked out the door.

It helped that I traveled. It gave us the break we needed from each other.

━━━

Before arguments got too heated, I left Erika's house on the low. I had a safe house located on the east side of Milwaukee that she didn't know anything about. That was where I hid my weapons, money, and other shit, and whenever she kicked me out, I went there, not a hotel.

I sipped a Canada Dry ginger ale and let the thoughts swirl through my head. Erika was a special kind of crazy that I loved so fucking much. She started a fight for sex. She liked how I roughly pushed her against the wall and grabbed her hair. I was aggressive but not abusive, and she loved that type of treatment. One and the same, making love was an art when with someone you loved.

Hard between the legs, I finished my drink and headed back to her crib. I called it her crib because she had the right to kick me out. Without prior relationship experience, all the shit I went through with Erika was new. I'd be lying if I didn't say her bomb pussy was a reason for my investment. Women came a dime a dozen, yet Erika was like special chocolate that was rare to taste.

By the time I walked through the door, her ass had been waiting on me. Just like all of the other times, we had bomb ass make up sex followed by a blunt. Time spent with Erika became a dream come true, but I had to make sure I kept my focus. It was imperative not to display vulnerability; a weakness women used to their advantage. Although I didn't believe Erika would, I moved forward cautiously.

CHAPTER 18

TYREE LYONS

PARKED two cars down from my target, I couldn't wait for the fun to begin. Chico was a creature of habit and had no idea I'd been following him for at least a week. I studied his patterns and movements, observing everything in great detail. He frequented a corner store by his crib on the north side, a two-story house, and his place of employment. The shit grew boring but eventually got interesting when Erika told me about her girl, Keisha. I also started to follow Keisha, which led me to a little hotel. Unsure of Keisha's motives, I wondered if she somehow was spying for him, but Erika assured me otherwise.

I didn't care for Keisha because that bitch was a home-wrecker, I couldn't respect that shit. However, she was Erika's friend, so out of love for her I kept my comments to myself. The second I noticed Keisha strut up to the door, I got out of the car and crossed the street. Lagging behind her, I kept my cell phone in hand as I slipped my left hand in my pocket. I smoothly slid a wedding ring on my ring finger and slowly approached the front desk. With my charm, I tried to sweet talk the receptionist for some information to find out anything I could about Chico's room location.

"Excuse me, lovely lady, how are you doing on this fine day?" Right away, she blushed and quickly provided her undivided attention.

"Hello sir I'm well, thank you! How may I assist you today?"

"Well, I was trying to do something special for my wife with assistance from her best friend. I wanted her room to be right next to her friend on the same floor. However, there is an issue," I confessed with a disappointed face.

The tall blonde haired woman asked puzzled, "How so?"

Right as I was about to explain, Chico strolled inside. Thinking quickly, I put my index finger up and put the phone to my ear. I took a few steps aside when I noticed Chico headed to the front desk. Within eavesdropping distance, I heard him ask for more bath towels to be sent to room 421. Instead of heading to the elevators, he went out of the door with Keisha. That fool had just given me exactly what I needed. I put the phone in my pocket and went back to the front desk.

"You won't believe this," I said to her trying to look disappointed. "That was my wife, and she won't be able to make it after all. Guess my surprise will have to wait."

"Oh bummer," she said.

"I guess it all worked itself out so I will just get a room for myself. Preferably something on the fourth floor," I added.

"Absolutely, let me check to see what's available. Did you want a smoking or nonsmoking room?"

"Smoking, thanks."

I gave her a debit card to hold for the room charges, and

she handed me a key. In the process of checking into the room, Erika hit my line, but I couldn't talk until I was alone. I took the stairs to the fourth floor all while I assessed the camera locations, hallway, and surroundings. I did the same thing once inside the room as I dialed Erika back.

"What up, baby?"

"Baby, please don't hurt my friend. She is completely innocent. She had no idea Chico was using her to get close to us. I really believe her too."

Something in Erika's voice told me to trust her.

"We good. I promise she will be alright. Love you, baby! I gotta go now. See you soon!"

"One love, baby," she said then hung up.

I took the stairs back down to the lobby. I went to my car to seize the large suitcase, careful not to run into the enemy. Back to my room, I began to set up shop. Unsure of how I wanted to kill him, I took a few pictures of the room before moving furniture around. Then I took one of the pillows and used my own pillowcase. By the time I finished, the entire room had been covered in plastic, and I was ready for that fool as nigga.

⊏⊐

I patiently waited for the right time to strike and took a chance and went to my car to hit my blunt and Black n' Mild and went back inside. The powers that be aligned the stars that night because we ended up crossing paths on my way back inside. The stairwell and elevator location was at the opposite ends.

"Nigga watch yo' self," Chico said, bumping into me without concern for his life.

To get him closer to my room, I indulged in his game for

a minute with a little back and forth. "Nigga, you better watch yo step before you get hurt. You young niggas are always running ya mouth."

"You got me fucked up my guy, so gone about your business. If I didn't have a chick waiting on me, I'd whoop yo' ass."

"Look I don't argue, so if you want to keep breathing, gone head into that room and calm down.

"You don't scare me, fool ass dude. I dare you to do something. You'll regret that shit on my mama who ever that bitch is!" he spat back at me.

Chico took the bait and kept running his mouth, moving closer and closer to room 415. As soon as he made it within reaching distance, I snatched his ass inside and closed the door. With a hard right hook, I decked his ass twice causing him to fall. I tied him to the two armed chairs. A glance down at my hands reminded me to slip on a pair of latex gloves.

"Damn, what the fuck?" Chico held his jaw trying to figure out what hit him.

"Yeah, I shut yo' ass up real quick," I remarked.

"Just wait until I get loose. You betta kill me. Otherwise, your ass is grass."

"Oh, you gonna die, don't worry. I'm the last nigga you will see before you meet your maker."

"Did that punk ass nigga Money send you? Huh, his punk ass can't fight his own battle after taking my girl!" Chico spat literally.

"I'm here for one reason nigga, Erika Cain. That name should ring a bell?"

His eyes bulged out as the wrinkles on the forehead followed. Both telltale signs, he knew it was a wrap. Ready to put him out of his misery, I made sure my words marinated into his head.

"Always be careful choosing friends because by association it can cost you your life. Don't worry though; Bishop's life will expire by my hands too. Erika sends her love, nigga."

I grabbed the pillow with the pillowcase and used it to suffocate him. Hands still tied up he didn't put up much of a fight as he wiggled until his last breath. While Chico's limp body sat slumped in the chair, I tried to figure out how to get his ass out of the room. Cutting him up would've taken too long not to mention the messiness. Then a light bulb went off in my head as my eyes continuously diverted to the extra-large suitcase.

I untied Chico's arms, drug him to the floor, and went to work breaking bones. To fit him inside, I broke the bottom two ribs and both shoulder blades to crunch and crossed his arms. Once he was in a fetal position, I took up all of the plastic and packed him inside the suitcase. Next, I moved all of the furniture back to its original spot then took a seat. A nigga was tired as hell. Before removing the gloves, I glanced around the room one last time making sure everything had been left in its place. Per departing the room, I tried to think of a dump site to dispose of the suitcase.

CHAPTER 19

ERIKA CAIN

MORNINGS WITH TYREE were the best because he always woke up with a stiff beef stick. I threw my lips around it and gave him the best head that I could to please him. While I played with his dick, it got me to thinking about all the hoes that got their ass whipped for a piece of meat. Bitches would do anything for the dick. I slurped and licked his chocolate stick until he became vocal then removed my mouth to avoid swallowing his kids.

"Damn, I love the way you say good morning to me, baby! You are priceless to me, girl. C'mon let's go shower so that I can return the favor."

Simultaneously we rolled out the bed and headed straight to the bathroom. Already naked, I stepped in the walk-in shower first and turned on the water wetting my hair. When I turned around, Tyree stood before me like the golden child with his yellow skin and tattoos.

"You so fucking beautiful," he said and joined me.

He took a soft washcloth and lathered it with Dove gentle exfoliating body wash and gently washed me. Unlike anything I'd ever let a man do to me, he had my heart no lie.

Each moment with him was a new experience that made me love him more. Once he thoroughly cleaned me, I returned the favor and then it got hot and heavy. He turned me around, placed my hands on the wall, and slide inside me. That position didn't last long, so I switched and bent over on the bench.

"Ohh shit, that feels so good. Aye, let's go back to the bed. I want to ride my shit."

I turned the water off and wrapped up in a bath towel and patted dry, ready to fuck the soul from his body. He laid flat on his back while his black stallion waited to penetrate my pussy. I climbed on top in the reverse cowgirl position to give him a view of my yellow ass. I straddled him with my knees on each side of his hips and slowly went up and down. I then changed it up, gyrated back and forth, in circles, and played with his dick using my pussy muscles.

"Fuck me! Oh shit, fuck me, baby!" he yelled and smacked my ass.

As I grind on him, I played with his balls, making his toes curl. After a while, I grew tired and switched off my knees and squatted over him with my feet flat on the bed. That position turned into doggy style, which happened to be one of my favorite ways to end our sexcapades. Tyree had a tight hold of my waist as he pounded in and out, giving me top notch dick. On the verge of releasing all my juices, he let my waist go and grabbed hold of my breasts.

"Ahh, shit!"

"I love you, Erika!"

"I love you too! More than you'll ever know, baby."

━━━

Intimacy and the power of the dick blew my mind each

time we shared each other's body. Tyree possessed a certain charisma that no other man had. It was like I was drowning in his love or under a spell of some kind. So in love with him, I loved his voice, touch, smell, and the crazy side. I never knew a love like this before with a man. Tyree had to be the first man I ever wanted to be with 24/7.

Alone for so long, I learned the meaning of love and being a ride or die chick. Although it was new at first, it all grew on me. Our bond had grown so much that it's hard to see myself without him now. He was the only man that made me feel comfortable enough to be me. I didn't have to hide anything from him. Ironically, we clicked so well yet butted heads because we shared the same birthday. But due to his profession, he traveled enough, which gave us space apart. I also had Keisha to chat with when he went away.

Once Tyree moved in, my communication with Keisha fell off to the point she insinuated that I changed. It wasn't something I did intentionally. The truth is, I was finally happy with life overall and kept busy. Despite that, our friendship remained strong, and we both agreed to make time for each other. She was the only girlfriend I had had, so our relationship was important to me. Being consumed in a man wasn't healthy, and Keisha made sure to remind me often. Blinded by love, all I wanted to do was cater to the nigga who touched my soul.

Moving forward, I became a ghetto Betty Crocker because I cooked and baked often to keep my man fed. Once he moved in, I gave up all of the fast food and prepared home-cooked meals. I cooked everything from collard greens, fried zucchini, and mac and cheese to desserts like cheesecake and peach cobbler. Tyree grew appreciative of my cooking so much so that he gained a few pounds. I did too, but in my backside from his good loving.

We complemented each other so well that it was almost like a dream. The longer we lived together, the more we learned about one another.

Life wasn't always fine and dandy when we had disagreements about shit. Both us of tended to be strong headed not wanting to back down. At times, I tried him just to see how far I could push him, but I learned to pick my battles. Whenever he clenched his jaw either he would leave the house, or I'd retreat to the smoking room. He killed for a living and I sure as hell didn't want to trigger that switch. Some might think I have a screw loose, and it's probably true, but makeup sex with Tyree made me feel like a pornstar giving my best performance.

———

I woke up with an attitude for no reason but realized it was the ending of the month. That bitch Aunt Flow was hanging around the corner. I got out of bed and took care of my hygiene and then went downstairs. Tyree was dressed and positioned in his favorite chair with his skull head mug.

"Hey, baby!"

"Good morning, love!"

I shuffled over to the Keurig machine and swiveled the K-Cup carousel looking for a Nutty Caramel Donut Shop, but there wasn't any left. In my feelings, I settled for a Dunkin' Donut Hazelnut. When I lifted the lid of the machine, there sat the K-Cup my taste buds craved for.

"Dang yo' black ass drunk my coffee. Please make sure to replace it. You know how I am about my coffee!" I spat.

"Really? Don't come at me for some damn coffee. You act like it'll kill you to drink something else."

"Well, buy more or don't touch the last flippin' cup!" I barked.

"Alright, I'm out. You are starting shit over a punk ass K-Cup. I'll be back," he hissed and strolled out the kitchen.

When Tyree and I had arguments, I acted petty as hell. This time he left the house to avoid physical confrontation. I cleaned the house from head to toe and sprayed some Glade Cashmere Woods air freshener. That shit smelled like a man's cologne, a guaranteed way to make him mad. Not even ten minutes afterward, he walked through the door.

"Erika, you really want me to fuck you up, right? Please don't tell me you had a nigga in my house."

"This is our house, playa. And if I did?" I questioned back with my hands on my hips. His blank and emotionless stare let me know he was still pissed off.

"I'm going to choke the fuck out of you and put a bullet in that nigga's head."

"Well, I'm glad there is no nigga. I sprayed this damn air freshener, fool," I said and retrieved the can to show him. He didn't believe me until he smelt it.

"Why you always playing and shit, you know I'm crazy as fuck. Stop doing that for real."

"You're too serious all the time, that's why. It's time you learned how to live a little. All you do is kill people and fuck me good. You gotta have fun and let loose, baby. I understand your childhood was fucked, but you gotta live and not just exist."

I walked closer and wrapped my arms around his neck as he embraced me. Ready for makeup sex, I kissed his soft lips and nibbled on the tip of his ear. I knew what was about to happen next.

"C'mon, let's go to the bedroom so I can slang this dang-a-lang on you, girl."

"You said the magic words, boo! I'm ready to get my ass smacked!"

"I never knew it was a woman out in the world just for me. You are perfect, baby. I know it's not easy loving a broken man like me with the baggage."

Well-deserved space from each other for an hour or two made him come home with a different attitude. For some reason, we as women had a bad habit of pushing a man to his limit just because we could. I liked to push his button from time to time for bomb ass sex. Free of diseases, we took annual tests for all STDs, including AIDS/HIV out of caution. That level of trust brought us closer, not to mention we fucked like rabbits.

Tyree laid it down so good that Mother Nature came and took me out of commission for a few days. Tyree hated to be around me and made sure he kept his distance; I didn't blame him one bit either. He took a trip to Chicago. Time away became a good thing for both of us. During that break, I did a lot of reflecting and sleeping.

CHAPTER 20

BISHOP WHITE

I MUST HAVE CUT over thirty heads within the past week, and it helped keep me occupied. The month of November tended to be busy, so when a few knuckleheads came in with no money, I usually hooked them up. They helped clean the shop as a payoff. I mainly did it for single moms who struggled to make ends meet. After all, small haircuts added up. That had been one way I gave back to the youngins in the neighborhood. Whenever a boy sat in my seat, I gave him words of wisdom— shit that somebody should've told me at their age.

From experience, young black men aren't taught certain shit during their upbringing due to a disruptive household. Unfortunately, they turn to the streets in search of all the shit they lack at home. Once the street life has sucked them in, nine times out of ten, they become a career criminal before seventeen years old. The lack of parenting nowadays is just as bad as in the 80s if not worse with that heroin and meth. Thankfully, Big Ma was there to teach me the life-long surviving essentials to make it in the world.

That's why once I got released from jail, I made myself

a promise to give back and help the youth. Locked behind bars had me reevaluating a lot of shit in life because I lost time that could never be replaced. Among things lost over time included finding love. Here I am a thirty-three-year-old nigga looking for love and then Erika Cain appeared. She made me feel alive and hopeful again. A hard knock life once taught me that love didn't love anybody. That shit was true as a muthafucka.

I chilled solo after work with a drink in my hand and some smoke. It had become a ritual of mine as a way to unwind. Feeling tipsy from the Hennessey, my thoughts drifted. I tried to figure out why women did the things they did. At my house on several occasions, we Netflix and chilled, but Erika never showed interest to take the next step. I had also been the perfect gentleman to and around her. Eventually, she told me it couldn't go any further than friendship between us. She also revealed her mutual dislike for Chico and my sister. At that point, all I could do was disconnect from her as she wished. I should have known something was up when she insisted on driving herself for our date.

After Erika basically dismissed my ass, I felt lead on and didn't appreciate it. She made me think we could build something together. Chico was right about her, but it was just another lesson learned. I guess finding my true love didn't exist for niggas like me. Drowning my sorrows in liquor, the sound of the doorbell made me snapback from la la land. Reluctant to move from the La-Z-Boy, I did a slow walk and shuffled my feet to the door.

"What the hell are you doing here? You said I was dead

to you the last time you were here." I spat just like a bitter nigga.

"Yeah, I know. We gotta talk about something though. You gonna let me in?"

Despite my feelings, I invited her inside to see what she had to say. When she stepped inside into the lighted area, her bruises became very visible. I truly felt bad for putting hands on her. That person no longer existed. A woman beater was nothing to be proud of. I did many things in life and never did it consist of physical abuse. I tried to apologize to Erika, but she went in on my ass without so much as batting an eye. For the first time I saw a different side to her, aggressive and full of misplaced anger.

"I don't want an explanation from yo bitch ass. I thought you were a cool person, but you crossed the line when you raised your hand. Not one woman in my family ever let a man hit them, and I'm no different."

"Look, I told you I'm sorry about what I did because it was out of line. What more do you want from me?"

"I don't want anything. I just needed to get that off my chest. You about to die, nigga."

When those words rolled off her tongue, a black James Bond looking ass dude sneaked into the room with his .9mm pointed at me. Before I could make a move, he walked behind me with the gun at my head. I couldn't believe what the fuck had just happened. That bitch set me up, and all I could do was stand still.

I remained cocky and stood stern, ready for whatever even with a gun pointed at me. Without warning, he knocked the shit out of me with the butt of the gun. He then proceeded to hit me a few more times before he finally spoke.

"So you like to put your hands on women, huh?"

Whoop!

"My girl's face is bruised because you felt the need to teach her a lesson. Guess what? It's your turn!" the suave nigga yelled as he pistol-whipped me.

Whoop! Whoop!

I felt the blood gush every time the gun made contact with my face. Numb from the continuous blows, my perfect vision soon turned blurred. However, I was able to see Erika. She watched as her man beat the shit out of me and didn't show one ounce of remorse. It should have made sense that light-skinned bitches couldn't be trusted. In and out of consciousness, all I could think about was my siblings and Big Ma.

We never know when our time will come. Shit, I sure as hell didn't. I guess the saying "Don't do to others what you don't want to be done to you" is true as hell. There I was unable to defend myself. I laid on the floor and soon went unconscious into the darkness. Just like spoiled meat, my expiration date had come, and I was tossed aside like garbage.

CHAPTER 21

ERIKA CAIN

NEITHER OF US had uttered a word about the October night our bond became unbreakable. That night replayed in my head often, more than I cared. I had never let a man lay hands on me. He signed his death warrant as a result of his actions.

Never had I seen Tyree in rare form, it meant a lot to know he cared about me. My nigga was crazy as hell. He wasn't a punk about his. It still boggled my brain that I took part in beating Bishop. It had been hard not to have flash-backs no matter how hard I tried to forget. Night time when I tried to turn my mind off seemed to be when the visuals tended to pop up.

At first, I reconsidered and didn't want to hit him as the blood blended into his jet-black beard. He looked at me through his right eye, his left one swollen closed. Suddenly the condition of his face gave me a flashback of my own. With all my might and strength, I struck the hell out the right side of his jaw.

Tyree took the gun back from me inside of a black cloth bandana. Once he cleaned the blood off, he twisted on the silencer. That was the first time I'd ever done anything so malice and it sure wasn't my last. Afterward, we exited the same way we entered without any contact with people. We made a clean getaway all the way back to our home.

―――

Drowning in his love, I wasn't in my right mind, and the crime that I helped him commit would forever stick with me. Whenever we were together, time stood still, Tyree was truly my best friend. Call me crazy, but I was Harley Quinn, and he was Joker. My mother had probably turned in her grave by my recent actions. Nevertheless, I had to live my life for me; I didn't have time to waste.

A week before Thanksgiving the stores were all packed with crazed folks who decided to shop at the last minute. I roamed and pushed my cart around Pick N' Save filling it with unnecessary shit. I wanted to make sure that I had everything before. It was the first holiday to be excited about in a long time because Tyree came into my life. Eighty bucks later, I carried the bags to the car, not paying attention to my surroundings. That day I learned never to let my guard down when you least expect it karma comes to bite ya in the ass.

My karma finally caught up to me in the blink of an eye as Bishop's sister Deja approached me. Her voice was the last thing I expected to hear, but there she stood in the flesh pissed. My heart pounded rapidly while the deranged woman stared me down.

"Bitch, where is my brother? He is not answering his phone!" she shouted as the gap between us slightly closed.

"I don't have a clue where he is right now and doesn't care. Hopefully, he lost my number too."

"Save the smart shit. You know where he's at. I can feel it. I've never liked you, and it's obviously for a reason. This is yo last chance trick," she threatened as she pulled out a gun.

"For the last time, I don't know!" The words left my lips during the same time she aimed and started firing shots.

The first few bullets strayed past me. Without hesitation, Deja walked up to me, not taking her finger off the trigger. Everything stood still as the loud sounds paralyzed me where I stood. I quickly tossed the bags in the backseat all the while trying to grab my phone. When I opened the driver door suddenly, I collapsed to the ground. Unaware a few bullets hit me; I lay on the pavement as the sounds of people screaming around me faded in and out. A voice came to me clear as day. It was such a sweet and soft voice. It was my mother.

Baby girl, what have you gotten yourself into? You have made me so proud of you for the good things you've done with the money I left you. Nevertheless, you know damn well I didn't raise your ass to be out here taking bullets and shit. That nigga must be something else for you to be lying and being tracked down by a mad woman. Erika, you are a grown woman, so you know right from wrong. It's not your time to join me yet. Your purpose on earth has not been fulfilled. I know you miss me because I miss you with all my heart, but in due time we'll be reunited again! Right now, mama needs you to fight and push through. Fight baby, fight baby, and wake up ERIKA!

"Erika, wake up! Can you hear the sound of my voice?"

The sound of a man's voice echoed as my eyelids fluttered open and closed. I fought hard to open my eyes again long enough to notice white people around me. Unaware of what happened, I tried to sit up but couldn't. In panic mode, two sets of hands held me down.

"It's okay. You're safe! My name is Tom, and I am a paramedic. You are in an ambulance in route to the hospital. Can you understand my words? Raise a finger if you can hear me," he said calmly in an effort to keep me from moving.

Puzzled as to what caused me to end up in that state, I mustered enough strength to lift my thumb in response. Trying not to move, Tyree was all I could think about as panic began to set in all over again.

"Erika, are you still with me dear? Hang in there. The doctors will take good care of you," Tom assured me.

He kept talking to me in an effort to keep me conscious. Unable to speak, all I could do was watch paramedics work on me. The sirens suddenly turned off as the ambulance stopped and the doors flung open. That was all I could remember before everything went black for the second time.

<hr/>

When I came around again, I felt groggy and sore, unable to move. Reality kicked in as my blurred vision allowed me to scan my surroundings. I realized I was in a hospital room, which also explained the high feeling. Unable to recall how I ended up there, a familiar voice gave me comfort.

"Hey, baby, I'm here," Tyree quietly comforted me.

CHAPTER 22

TYREE LYONS

I RUSHED TO AURORA ST. Luke's Hospital after the call from a lady who witnessed Erika get shot. She gave me detail for detail as I stepped on the gas pedal. Somehow I blamed myself because the whole family should've been eliminated after Bishop. Never had I been a big religious person, but I silently prayed that Erika's life was spared. Inside the hospital, I stopped the first nurse I saw to inquire information on Erika's whereabouts. Within ten minutes

"Hey, baby! I'm here," I said, holding her hand. A smile crept across my face when Erika's eyes flickered. I thought she was going to die.

"How is she, Doc?"

"The first bullet made a shored exit through her forearm. The tight shirt and jacket she wore helped. The second bullet hit her abdomen causing her to lose a lot of blood. Good news, there is no internal bleeding. Ms. Cain is a fighter. We removed the entire slug without damaging any major organs."

"Anything major we should be concerned about?" I

question the doctor as he provided answers to each question.

"She should recover just fine. We will continue to monitor her blood and urine tests to keep an eye out for infections and kidney functions. No other surgeries will be needed from my observations."

"Thank you so much, doctor!" Elated, I couldn't contain my smile as I never continued to hold Erika's hand.

"Don't stay too long. She needs to get rest. I'll make sure to phone you if her condition changes."

"There's no need," I quickly replied. "I'll know if something goes wrong. Thank you again, and have a good night." I extended my hand in a gesture for a handshake before he walked away.

"Tyree, what happened to me? Why do I feel different right now," she asked, still loopy from the medication.

"That crazy bitch Deja shot you outside the grocery store. A bystander witnessed it all. During the commotion, your phone fell out. She took a wild guess, found my number, and called me, but you are alive, that's all that matters." I placed a kiss on my forehead.

"Wwwhhhaaattt! I never liked that trick," she joked which let me know she was lucid.

"Yeah, she shot you twice. It doesn't even matter because I'm about to handle her and her family.

She stopped talking and pointed to the white Styrofoam cup that sat on the serving tray. I assisted her as she took a few sips of water. I noticed the cup was cold, which indicated the nurse had recently been there. Rather than resume my questions, I fluffed her pillow, kissed her on the forehead again, and made plans to visit her the next day. Once Erika's room door closed behind me, I was ready to end Deja's life. I got sloppy somehow and forgot all about her only because of the heavy focus on Chico. That bitch caught Erika in broad daylight, and the timing couldn't have been worse. It's Thanksgiving, a rare moment to be thankful for someone, and a bitch tried to take my heart from me.

⊏══⊐

Ready to erase Bishop's family from the face of the earth, my goal was to destroy shit. I contacted a friend who owed me a favor to locate every member of Bishop's family. Deja fucked with the wrong woman, and the only way to get even was to eliminate their entire bloodline. The true grim reaper and beast inside of me had awakened. It was as if something in my head triggered.

I drove to my safe house, gathered weapons, and filled my duffle bag then headed to a chop shop. Around the corner from my spot, the nigga who owned it was into all types of shady shit so I knew he would be down to make extra cash. It had gotten dark outside, but the lights illuminated the area as I did a slow drive into the lot. Lights were also on from what appeared to be the office that prompted me to park and exit. Two pistols accompanied me along the walk just in case I had to lay a nigga out. To my surprise, the door opened, and that's when I noticed the camera mounted above me.

"What it do? Who you here to see, my nigga?" a big dude barked as he stood in front of me. He looked like that big nigga Goldmouth from the movie *Life* who whooped Eddie Murphy for his cornbread.

"What up. I need to holla at Dino for a minute. He's not expecting me, but we have a mutual friend in common."

"And who the fuck is that?"

To keep from fucking his big ass up, I took a deep breath

in and gradually exhaled before I responded. "Cash mutha-fucking money. Now if you don't mind letting me in or getting Dino. I got somewhere important to be and time ain't waiting, you feel me?"

Patiently I waited until another male's voice grew closer to the door.

"Slim, what the fuck? You ain't left yet? Get yo ass to the east side before that bitch disappears. Aye," he stopped talking long enough to stare me down as I did the same. "What you need, my nigga?"

"I got some business to handle, but my car and plates can't be identified. You got something to help a nigga out?"

"It depends on what you looking for and how much money you got."

I tossed his ass two racks, which shut him up. He motioned his finger as I followed to the area where the vehicles were. It was about three other niggas working and talking shit to each other. When we hit the corner, and the first thing I saw was a damn Charter Communications Cable vehicle. It was exactly what I needed to do surveillance.

"I'll take that," I pointed at it not even wondering why he had it in the first place.

"That bitch belongs to you now. It's clean, the plates are legit, and the key is inside the glove compartment. Aye, I'm not gonna ask what you about to do, but be smooth. I don't know you, and you don't know me, aiight?"

"Word. Good looking, my nigga! One more favor, can you have one of yo' boys park it and cover it outside? I'll be back to snatch it and be out."

"Done."

"Holla black," I stated as I escorted myself out the way I came in.

Around ten-thirty the next morning, I was still in kill mode, ready to snap Deja's neck or worse. Her brother was the reason all this shit popped off the way it did, but I blamed myself most of all. Falling in love was new. It distracted me from protecting myself. All a nigga knew how to do was kill, and I had begun to worry Erika would slowly change me. It wasn't until she got shot that I realized she had already changed me.

Just as I was about to retreat and try again later, the window of Deja's apartment opened. I started the engine and drove around the block before I parked across the street from her building. In a Charter Communications shirt and hoodie Dino left for me, I climbed out the truck, grabbed two orange cones, and dropped one in the front and back of the truck. I then got some equipment from the back. I calmly crossed the street all while watching my surroundings. Up three flights of stairs and a long hallway, the adrenaline pumped through my body. Multiple scenarios played through my head as to how the situation would play out.

I knocked and announced myself, and then I pulled out a pair of shoe covers and slipped them on. When the door opened, our eyes locked instantly. I had the enemy right where I wanted her, scared and thrown off. My plan to catch her off guard worked, it momentarily threw off her thinking process. Her shifty eyes couldn't believe my appearance. Deja wore a worried face as she stood face to face with karma.

"Get yo ass back and don't be stupid!" I ordered and stepped inside as I used my foot to close the door behind me.

An unbreakable gaze between the two of us had me

spacing because there was evil staring back at me. I saw the lump form in her throat as she swallowed. She froze with a cold gaze at the .9mm pointed at her.

"Who the fuck are you?"

Whoop!

"Watch your mouth, bitch!"

I slapped her across the face with my gun and was glad there was no bloodshed. She stumbled back and quickly raised her hand to her face. Wide-eyed that I hit her, she stood stunned. In a short time, I made a mental map in my head of how shit looked before I arrived in the apartment.

"Sit yo ass in that chair and don't make me say it more than once. You were the big bad bitch with the gun when you shot my girl. I got the gun now, so do what you're told or get filled with holes."

"Nigga, you don't scare me. Do you know who my brother is?"

"Past tense, bitch. Do I know who your brother was?" I corrected her. I retrieved a pair of latex gloves from my back pocket. "Get ya ass in the chair!"

"What?" she momentarily froze with bulging eyes. "You a lie. My brother wouldn't dare let a nigga catch him slipping!" her disbelieving voice spat.

"Cuff each hand to the arms." I tossed her two sets of silver handcuffs with one hand while my piece remained aimed.

"What the hell did you and that bitch do to my brother? I knew he shouldn't have brought her around."

"I know you better cuff yourself," I ordered as I used my free hand to assist. "Aye, you really want to know? I killed yo punk ass brother for putting his hands on my girl. He got pistol whipped by my bitch and me just like I'm about to do you for being disrespectful."

"Fuck!" she spat at me, literally. I slapped her ass for doing that nasty shit. She had really pissed me off beyond no control.

"I knew y'all had something to do with his disappearance. My grandma has been sick about that shit too. Karma will get yo ass sooner than later no matter what you do to me."

"Tell that shit to your brother when you see his ass, but before I send you off, how many more of you are left?" Deja frowned in confusion by my question, so I clarified. "Every member of your family will die by my hands."

Her facial features slightly resembled those of her deceased brother. Distracted by her gray eyes, I quickly caught myself.

"Any last words you want me to share with your grandma?"

"I have a few last words but they ain't for my grandma, nigga. They are for you. I want them to replay in your head at night."

"Watch yo mouth!" I warned in a stern tone, but her ass kept talking anyway.

"When I shot Erika, it felt good because I never liked her. She fucked with my brother's head, so she had to pay. Please know that it gave me satisfaction. The scared look on her face was priceless. If my aim were better, your sweet girl would've taken a bullet to the head."

"Bitch!" I yelled, enraged from her words. I let three bullets in her ass, one in the head execution style, and two in the gut. My silencer muffled the noise as Deja's body went still, and her head fell low.

Nobody noticed me leave her apartment. I got the fuck out ASAP and drove the truck miles away from Deja's location. In route, there was a deserted junkyard with a bunch of abandoned cars. The area was a perfect dump site. I parked it and climbed out with a black duffle bag still wearing gloves. I checked my surroundings then went to the back of the truck. I quickly changed shirts and shoes then tossed the old stuff inside, then doused everything down with lighter fluid, and lit it up. Like a smooth criminal, my presence went unnoticed, and a nigga went ghost.

CHAPTER 23

TYREE LYONS

I STROLLED through the hospital feeling ten times better knowing that another enemy had met her maker. Deja crossed the line, and she had to die. It had been a while since I felt refreshed and content. The closer I got to Erika's room, the more excited I became to see her. The door was partly cracked open, I walked inside, and before I could speak, she spoke first.

"Afternoon, baby!" she greeted.

"Hey! How did you know it was me?"

"You are wearing that Dolce & Gabbana Intenso cologne I bought you. For some reason, my sense of smell is off the chart."

"Damn, you good! How are you feeling? You are looking better." I tried to boost her spirits.

"Today is better than yesterday, but when can I go home? I'm so ready to sleep in my own bed." She ran her fingers through her hair with poked out lips.

"Whenever the doctor clears you, but until then, you gotta sit still, little mama. In due time, I'll be able to whisk you away from here," I joked.

"You're in a good mood. What has you so talkative?" I knew Erika would catch on soon, but I wanted her to focus on healing.

"A nigga is just glad to see you alive and well. I can't lose you, ma." I kissed her gently.

"You are such a romantic," she joked as a knock on the door ceased our laughter. Her doctor and nurse entered closing the door behind them.

"Well, it is pleasing to see you awake and laughing. How are you feeling today, Ms. Cain?

"Sore but well. I'm ready to go home. I assume you're here to tell us some good news."

"Actually I am. First, we wanted to look at your wounds, change the dressing, and chat about the healing process. You will be very limited on what you can do for a few more weeks."

"I'll do whatever I'm supposed to do, doctor. I just want some chicken and shrimp pasta, Netflix, and my bed." Everyone shared a chuckle, but Erika was dead serious.

The doctor proceeded with more questions about the living arrangement and precautions to take during the healing process. I stood beside Erika while the doctor gave specific instructions. I also watched the nurse's step-by-step process as she washed the wound and applied a clean bandage.

"Can you please avoid the stairs?"

Erika and I both answered yes at the same time. We looked at each other, smiled, and returned our attention to Dr. Garcia.

"Good. I'm going to prescribe you some antibiotics and Vicodin for the pain. You can shower but will need assistance. Please don't try to go back to your daily routine, not just yet." Dr. Garcia continued on about bandaging the wound among more do's and don'ts.

Afterward, the doctor and nurse exited the room as I assisted Erika in getting dressed. Caring for another human being had never been my forte, especially a woman, but Erika changed my whole perspective. She shined a light on my dark side, kept me balanced, so I owed it to her. I retrieved the comb and hairbrush I brought from home and did my best to brush her hair into a ponytail to the back.

"Damn bae, you really love me, huh? Thank you for helping take care of me. I still can't believe I got shot. That shit not cool at all."

"All you gotta do is focus on healing so that we can go away somewhere. What you think about that?" Before she could answer the door opened as the nurse pushed a wheelchair in the room.

"Let's get you out of here," she said while she locked the chair on each side.

I assisted Erika into the chair slowly careful not to hurt her in any way.

"Here are your discharge papers and prescriptions for the meds. If you notice swelling, more blood than usual, or anything unusual calls us."

"Thank you, ma'am, for everything. This little lady will take it easy and rest per the doctor's orders," I joked as I wheeled Erika through the halls of the lobby to the revolving doors.

The nurse stood with her while I retrieved my car a few steps away and returned. We proceeded to get Erika in the car, careful that the seat belt wasn't too tight around the stomach area.

"Home, here we come." I was so glad to drive away from that place with my queen.

The next morning, I sat in my man cave and finished a business deal for a new investment, a million dollar mansion located in Marietta, Georgia. After what happened to Erika, it was time for a change. Tired of the Midwest, we needed a new start in a new location. A gated home was a step up from how we were used to living. It was time to spend a little money and lay low with my rider. The mansion had everything from a tennis court to a home theater and gym.

Currently, almost seven a.m., I went upstairs to check on Erika and to make breakfast. When I approached the living room, she still had her eyes closed, looking like sleeping beauty. Peaceful and beautiful I stood and watched in awe until she caught me.

"Morning, baby boo! Why are you standing over me?"

"Sorry I just couldn't help it! I've missed you so much, and I'm glad to have you back with me," I confessed then sat next to her.

"I won't lie. I missed the shit out of you too. That hospital shit is for the birds, and I sure don't want to go back."

"You won't, not if I can help it. Speaking of which, I should tell you my latest plan. We're moving as soon as you get healed up. Here look at this and tell me what you think."

I pulled my phone out and showed her the mansion I'd purchased for us. As her thumb swiped across the screen, it became obvious that she was pleased with the pictures. Suddenly her mouth dropped open in surprise, and I knew exactly why.

"Tyree, you spent a million dollars? When did all of this happen?"

"Please don't concern yourself with the details baby,

just know everything is legit and we are getting up out of here."

"What made you pick the south? Do you know anyone in Georgia?"

"Nope. I figured a random place where no knows us would perfect for a fresh start. Don't you agree?"

While she continued to hold onto my phone, I made my way to the kitchen to cook. Slowly Erika followed me careful not to bump her stomach when she sat in the chair.

"What are you about to make us?"

"Pancakes or French toast with scrambled eggs and fruit. I want to get you full but not too full to disturb the stomach."

"Pancakes are fine; maybe three quarter sized ones! Now back to this moving stuff. I never knew you had plans, but I'm all in for it. I'm actually excited."

"Good. We're moving as soon as you are better. Start thinking about the shit you want to take along but note we are getting new furniture and everything."

"No arguments from me. However, I need to figure out how to manage the center. There are a lot of people who rely on the resources," she insisted.

While she talked, I moved around the kitchen and retrieved two medium-sized plates. The pancakes came out perfect in size, golden and fluffy, and so did the scrambled eggs with cheese.

"You worry too much, baby! I got all of that under control, just focus on getting back to normal. Here eat this and stop being a worry wart," I demanded sitting the plate and bottle of syrup in front of her."

We sat together and enjoyed breakfast, something we hadn't done in a very long time. So in love with the woman who sat across from me, I had to make her my wife sooner than later. She completed me.

Erika had healed up and slowly got back to her regular routine. I had even cut back on taking contracts because we were so focused on starting a new life. So much so, Erika ended up getting pregnant, which became a life changer for us. Our timetable to move happened early enough to move and settle into the mansion. Used to moving solo, I had to grow accustomed to taking care of two other human beings. Eventually, I grew more and more acceptable of the new chapter, I was ready to take the next step. I was ready to make Erika my wife.

CHAPTER 24

ANTOINETTE

REFRESHED AND WELL RESTED, I decided to wake up before Breya and Money to make breakfast. Movie night turned into a freak fest filled evening among the three of us. Although I had agreed to join Money and Breya, in my head, I still felt conflicted. The act of performing oral sex on a woman would never happen. In no way did it never appeal to me, although I loved it done to me. Then again I never saw myself doing the shit I did last night either.

In a relationship with a man and woman simultaneously, had to be the craziest shit I'd ever done. No matter how hard I tried to resist joining Breya and Money in a polyamorous relationship, my body made the final decision. All awkwardness disappeared within the first few weeks, and things turned into a normal routine. The lifestyle had its challenges, but overall, it worked. To keep things fresh, I stayed at my place four days out of the week. I had a key to their place but always announced myself before popping up.

I'd finally accepted my new sexual orientation as a bisexual, something that would've been shameful to admit in the past. Although Chico gave me the best sex that will forever be a memory, Breya and Money were better. The two gave me intimacy on another level, one I didn't know existed. Throughout being with them, we grew to learn each other's bodies. The three of us had an understanding, and no one had to lie about what went on. The once toxic dealings I went through with Chico dissipated and were replaced with peace.

Throughout the breakup process from Chico, I learned a lot about myself as a woman and person in general. Meditation became a part of my daily routine, which helped me protect my peace. I learned that men like Chico would always cheat no matter how loyal their woman proved to be. I made a vow to appreciate myself and never let a man do me wrong as long as I breathed. Breya and Money also taught me it's okay to have fun and break societal rules.

When the bacon, sausage links, scrambled eggs, and biscuits were finished, my partners entered the kitchen with the biggest grin on their faces. We were basically roommates with benefits. Plates and silverware were already laid on the island counter along with two Anchors large glass jars. One was filled with ice cold water and the other with low pulp Tropicana orange juice.

"Good morning, sleepy heads! Take a seat, you're right on time for breakfast," I said while I placed the food on a large plate.

"Man, everything smells so good! I'm starving too. Last night got me famished," Money confessed and then kissed me on the cheek. He took a seat all while letting out a yawn.

"Netta, you didn't have to do all of this. How long have you been up?"

"Girl, this is nothing! My stomach woke me up a little

after five. I figured I'd get up early enough to have coffee and cook for y'all."

"Thank you! Next time I'll cook for everyone. As a matter of fact, how does corn beef sound for lunch?"

"Hell yeah! I can taste that shit now," Money greedy ass blurted out. I watched while he loaded his plate with crispy bacon, sausage links, and biscuits.

Breya and I laughed and went on to fix our plates then sat at the kitchen table. In the process of enjoying our meal and each other's company, it hit me that my birthday was around the corner.

"Aye, my birthday's coming up. What are we gonna do?"

"Shit, whatever you want to do, baby! Name it, and we'll do it. But on another tip, breakfast was da bomb!"

"Sure was," Breya agreed. She slid her chair from the table and proceeded to clean the table. There weren't many dishes because I washed them as I cooked.

"I'm about to roll up these two blunts. Anyone joining me?"

"Hell yeah! I'm right behind you," both Breya and I replied at the same time then busted out in laughter.

While she quickly cleaned the kitchen, I followed behind Money ready to get my buzz on. Not even noon yet, all three of us smoked both blunts and watched *Mac & Devin Go to High School* with Snoop Dogg and Wiz Khalifa until the TV watched us.

Several hours later, I had showered, dressed, and left from Money and Breya's home. There were a few errands I needed to take care of before heading home. During my drive to Chase Bank, flashbacks of Chico popped in my head. I finally got him out of my system like a bad drug that weighed me down.

As the month went by I grew worried because my period was late and I realized Money didn't use a condom all the time. Each morning I woke up and rushed to the bathroom in hopes of seeing the red river flow but no luck, not to mention my breasts had grown tender. Hesitant to tell Money, I made a doctor's appointment for the following day. I prayed it was just my body changing. Lord knows a child was the last thing I needed at the moment. Anxious to find out what the hell was happening with my body, I decided to stay home and keep my distance from Money and Breya.

Thankfully the receptionist scheduled me for the earliest appointment possible. Unable to sleep through the night, I tossed and turned until the sun came up. I had turned into a nervous wreck over the entire situation. Dressed by seven a.m., I ate two Yoplait strawberry yogurts, along with a bagel lightly spread with strawberry cream cheese.

The doctor visit went faster than I anticipated, but the results were expected. The pregnancy tests had prepared me for the new reality, but hearing the words flat out scared me shitless. In the first trimester, the doctor provided me with a few prescriptions. She also suggested some apps I could download on my phone or Kindle to read about the process.

I sat with the phone in my hand for at least forty minutes while debating to call Money or text him. There was no way to know how he'd react to what I had to say. Either way, he needed to know that his life would forever change. My eyes glanced over the words I had typed I pressed send.

Me: *Hey, Bri! I just left the doctor and got some unexpected news, and I don't know what to do. I'm pregnant.*

Hit with cold feet, I wasn't sure how she'd react but figured she would understand the situation. On pins and needles, I gawked at the phone waiting for a reply. Finally, the gray bubbles popped up.

B: *Wow! That is crazy as hell, girl. Come over here right away because we need to have a conversation.*

Me: *I'm on my way. Did you tell Money already?*

B: *Not yet. But that isn't our only issue. We'll talk more when you get here.*

Me: *Okay. Be there soon.*

I sat there in dead silence as the nausea feeling stirred inside causing me to rush to the bathroom. Already tired of morning sickness, I stayed on the floor until nothing else came up. Afterward, I stood to my feet, rinsed my mouth, and then slapped cold water on my face. I proceeded to leave the house in route to my second home. The entire drive I recalled my actions and tried to prepare for the consequences. Not a person who wanted kids. It no longer mattered because an abortion never crossed my mind.

My stomach continued to nervously flutter as I exited my car in a movement towards the front door. With key in hand, I entered inside, but without notice, the smell of garlic hit my nose. Immediately my mouth watered from the pungent odor, I closed the door before hauling ass to the bathroom. Before I could step out, Breya stood in front of the door ready to ask fifty questions. For a minute, I wasn't sure what the hell she had in mind from the quiet psycho stare she wore.

"Money's not home yet. We need to talk first before letting him know what's up. There is something we need to discuss, woman to woman," she declared.

"Damn, too bad I can't have a damn drink for this shit," I joked.

CHAPTER 25

KENTRELL "MONEY" GIPSON

HAVING Netta around the house felt like a dream, but it was a reality. She made herself at home and had finally loosened up around Breya. I loved having both women around me because they kept shit copacetic. Netta cooked breakfast, and Breya helped clean up. I lived for the weekends to spend time with my ladies uninterrupted doing the simplest things. We went to the movies, dinner, concerts, and chilled at the crib all without drama. Two women at one time seemed impossible in the beginning, but Breya and Netta complemented each other well.

At times they clicked so well that it made me jealous of their bond. They would shower together and sleep next to each other as if they were Siamese twins. They became inseparable at times even though Netta had her own place. Women were one of God's best creations, and I was thankful to have two. Netta surprised me when she finally gave in and agreed to join our circle.

Our setup couldn't have been better, which turned out to be a win for everyone. I had two chicks to fuck anytime, and they had each other. The two got closer over time and even performed sexual acts without me. That shit became a muthafucking turn on. Within the first month, we fucked so much my stamina became an issue. My johnson couldn't keep up with both women as I hoped.

My shit got hard and all that, but I couldn't last long enough to fuck each woman equally. As a man, shit like that hurt my ego, but Breya and Netta never complained. They showed me that it didn't matter to them because what we had went beyond the physical aspect of the relationship.

My faulty equipment began to function properly again giving me my masculinity back. Never in life did I have issues performing sexually. I stopped drinking so much and ate more fruits and vegetables. Within a few weeks, my body had accepted the change, and I went back to slanging my meat on my ladies.

Ever since Breya got promoted at her job, it left me more time to spend with Netta. We bonded on another level other than sex. We talked about the good old days and reminisced. We laughed. She cried and even opened up more about her relationship with Chico. Each moment we shared alone, I fell more in love with her as if Breya didn't matter. Little did I know, Breya grew a bit jealous, and she had begun to let me know she felt some type of way about Netta. Breya claimed my obsession with another woman made her feel invisible at times. Sadly, I had to agree, Netta made my heart smile, my dick jump, and I felt like I did in high school.

As time moved forward, Netta kept her own place and refused to move in with us. She remained persistent that her space remains protected in case things went left in our relationship. I respected how she felt, so I never brought up the topic again. Deep down, it was for the best because my love for her grew more than I ever imagined. It got so bad that Breya began to notice it and called me out. Apparently, I'd been calling out Netta's name in my sleep for several nights which pissed Breya off.

Sleeping good as hell all of a sudden, I felt a big gush of warm liquid splash on me. At first, it felt like a dream, but then I heard Breya's voice as she hit me with the pillow. When I opened my eyes, she stood over me. My t-shirt wet, I grew pissed.

"Yo, what the fuck is wrong with you? Quit hitting me. Shit!"

"Nigga, you lied to me."

"About what? We tell each other damn near everything."

"Exactly. Damn near everything, which implies that it's one percent of shit you don't tell me about. Anyway, we have a situation on our hands, which involves both me and Netta."

What type of situation?" I asked and then moved to the edge of the bed. I removed the damp shirt over my head and tossed it on the bed.

"My period is late. It's almost been a month. The other crazy part of the story is that Netta is knocked up too."

"Say what?" I leaned my head in as if I didn't hear her clearly enough. "Knocked up? Are you sure?" In that split second, the front door closed and Netta appeared as if she heard her name mentioned.

"Hey y'all. From the looks of things, I imagined Bri told you already. I'm around four or five weeks along."

"Wow!" I sighed in disbelief.

Both women stood next to each other as their faces told

the same story. None of us expected the results, and of course, I was the biggest person to blame. Aware of the results from unprotected sex, it came with a price. In our case, two children were the result. In an effort to console them, I extended my arms out as a gesture.

"I'm not sure yet, but what if I am?"

"We have to plan together and move forward with life. This might not be what we planned, but neither of you is getting an abortion. The living arrangement has to get worked out too. I feel we should all live under the same roof."

"This shit is wild. What are the odds?" Breya expressed stunned. She stood up from the bed to retrieve the blunt that I had rolled earlier. Out of the blue, Netta jumped up and ran towards the bathroom. Stuck on not knowing what to do, I snatched the blunt from Breya. She snatched the bitch right back and took a few drags.

"What the fuck?" I yelled at her.

"Nigga, calm down. It won't hurt. It's to help with nausea and queasiness. Google that shit," Breya spat.

Netta came back into the room and immediately motioned for the blunt. Without a word, she took three pulls, exhaled, and went to the living room. Naturally, I followed behind her in an effort to make sure she was okay. On the couch, I sat next to her but laid back and pulled her my way.

"Aye baby, are you okay? I know this is a lot, but I promise we'll get through it. Please forgive me I never meant for this to happen."

"It's not all your fault. I should've made sure you wore a condom, but we can't change anything now. They say everything happens for a reason. I'm just glad it's not Chico's child."

Before my words left my lips, I looked up to notice Breya standing a few steps away. Unable to notice her mood, I continued to rub Netta's shoulder as I blew Breya a kiss in the air. It didn't take long for her to join us in need of the same attention. She laid her head on me too. While the three of us chillaxed, it became very apparent that I had gotten myself into a sticky situation. I had to figure out how I would survive living with two pregnant women with raging hormones.

EPILOGUE

DESPITE THE GUNSHOT wound to my abdomen, all of the internal organs functioned well enough for me to get pregnant. It was hard to believe that Tyree and I conceived a baby. Experiencing pregnancy and giving birth had to be two of the craziest yet unforgettable moments besides being shot. Carrying a living human being inside of me meant we had to live for the sake of our child. Over the initial shock of life-changing events, I soon thought about the Leap of Faith Center. The organization meant the world to me, and to keep it running, I had to make a decision.

A day before moving, I visited my crew. They deserved an explanation before I left town. The topic of relocating was mentioned but never confirmed. Any other time I'd be glad to see Friday, in this case, I had to say goodbye to my small family. While patiently waiting for everyone to arrive that morning, I placed a card on each person's desk that had been filled with a fifty dollar bill and an Amazon gift card. Ms. Pam and Ms. Susan were the exceptions; they each received an extra hundred. Tyree sent me money via Cash App to purchase everything, including the money to fill the cards. His selfless gestures made my heart melt, and the main reason I'd agreed to leave Milwaukee.

While patiently waiting for everyone to trickle inside, I sat at my desk preparing file folders on the computer desktop. Each folder contained detailed information for invoices, vendors, contact numbers, and so on. I wanted to have electronic documents accessible for the new woman in charge. Not confident that Ms. Pam would accept the offer, she proved to be trustworthy.

"Ms. Erika Cain, I'm gonna get you, child," I heard the sweet voice of Ms. Pam as she appeared before me holding her card.

"Good morning! I'm glad you're here. Sit down please, I need to tell you something," I requested. She did as asked while she continued to read the text of the card. It hurt to fix my lips to tell her the news, but I went ahead so that we could share the moment.

"You are finally going to leave and start that new chapter away. I'm so proud of you," she rejoiced. Witnessing her smile and tears caught me off guard because I promised myself not to cry.

"Yes, ma'am. It's time to live while I have the chance. I want to thank you for encouraging me. Having you around has made the difference in how the Center runs. Therefore, I want to turn things over to you."

"Erika, no, I can't," she quickly objected.

"Umm, you don't have a choice, ma'am. Everything has been switched over. Tyree set up a fund that will cover the cost for everything each month. You've been the glue and mother figure, so it's only right you have this place. Of course, the rest of the crew will have responsibilities to fulfill."

I watched the overly joyful woman. Her natural beauty,

even in her early sixties, made me smile. Ms. Pam wore her salt and pepper hair in finger coils giving her a hip yet age-appropriate appearance.

"Bless your heart child. This is unbelievable. Let me try to calm down," she joked. We shared a laugh and hugged just as the sound of the door opened, followed by voices. We dried our eyes before we joined the others who were headed to their desks.

"Aww, this is so sweet! Erika, you are always doing nice stuff. Uh oh, is something bad about to happen?" Jen blurted. She had been a work in progress and the youngest of us.

Before making a speech, I waited until all the envelopes were opened. Overcome with sadness, I happily watched my family. They forever had a place in my heart no matter the distance.

"Now that you all have read your card and pocketed the cash, I'd like to just say a few words before we open for the day. This organization wouldn't be successful without your assistance. Thank you for taking a chance with me, for giving up time out of your day to help our brothers and sisters of the community. Ms. Pam will be graciously resuming in my absence, effective immediately."

"Wow, it's not going to be the same without you around.

I returned to the place I called home knowing that in twenty-four hours we'd be on the road. Still kind of emotional from my official departure from the Center, I let the emotions flow as I went from room to room letting the good and bad memories come over me. The idea of starting freshly provided flutters in my stomach. The ringing phone interrupted me as I reminisced. I retrieved it from my back pocket to see it was Keisha.

"Hey girl," I answered.

"What are you doing? We should go eat since y'all leaving in the morning. I'll even treat too."

"Umm, give me a few minutes; I'll meet you at Applebee's in Bayshore. Is that cool?"

"Alright, I'll see you soon," Keisha confirmed before we disconnected.

Keisha and I had a distance between us after the Chico situation. Tyree voiced his opinion of her; but of course I tried to defend my friend. Although I understood his position, I couldn't just cut Keisha off. Eventually, we came to a mutual understanding. As I walked back to my bedroom to gather my purse and keys, my phone went off again. This time it was Tyree checking in on me. I always loved getting messages from him no matter the time of day. After I replied to his text, I headed down the stairs and out of the door.

Half an hour later, I parked not realizing Keisha had parked two spaces down. I exited my vehicle careful to set the alarm. There had been a string of car thefts in the area lately. I followed behind a crowd of folks who were entering the restaurant. Not sure where my girl took a seat, I informed the host I was meeting someone. Luckily, Keisha had let him know she had been expecting another guest. The nice gentleman escorted me to the table before disappearing.

"Girl you are glowing," she acknowledged as she stood. We shared an embrace then took a seat.

"Thanks. I'm ready to eat," I insisted. It only took a few minutes to scan the menu before our server approached to take orders.

"So how are you feeling about the move? I can't believe

you leaving my friend. Things will not be the same, that's for sure," Keisha voiced.

"I'm still trying to believe it myself. I've never been this happy before and I love Tyree. I'll promise to keep in touch. What are you going to do?"

"Continue to run my shop and stack money. Eventually I want to relocate south somewhere. It's time for a new chapter; the last year has been beyond wild."

"I feel you. This city has changed and the violence has gotten ridiculous. I be damned if my baby grows up here. It's too crazy now."

"Whatever I do, I'll keep you posted. Shit, who knows, you might need me to fly out to do your nails," Keisha joked.

"Hmm, that might be a good idea," I agreed. Amid us joking, the server returned with our meal.

The two of us enjoyed our last meal together by going back down memory lane. We laughed, cried, and made each other a promise to stay in touch. I didn't have any girlfriends or anyone besides Tyree. Before we got inside our vehicles to depart, Keisha opened her trunk to retrieve a gift bag. The waterworks started right away.

"Erika you have been a good friend to me and this is just a small way to show my appreciation. I love you girl."

"Aww, bitch, you know I'm a crybaby. You didn't have to get me anything." We shared one last hug before going separate ways.

———

Our unborn child forced us to grow up and change our lifestyle. Tyree and I relocated to Marietta, Georgia for a new start. He eliminated the White family, which closed a chapter in his book. It took me time to accept his actions, but it wasn't anything I could've done to stop him. As a trained killer, I had no sway on him, so I turned my head to that part of his business. Eventually, his work lightened up, and in a sense, it improved him as a person. He used to tell me at night how killing drained him mentally. I prayed the move from Milwaukee would be another aide to assist him in the transition to fatherhood.

Still, with child, I agreed we go to the Cobb County Probate Court to obtain a marriage license. With no family, we didn't need a big lavish ass ceremony, just something simple and intimate. When the religious clergy member officially announced us, husband and wife, our kiss sealed the deal. Life as a wife and mother changed how I thought and did things. Responsibility had become my first name because both the husband and baby relied on me.

Tyree grew as a person during our time together. He opened up more and more, making himself vulnerable to me. He shared secrets and demons he faced, which helped me understand him better. Complex yet loveable, he tended to be misunderstood by those who didn't know him. It didn't matter though because we had each other, and that's all that mattered. When we said our vows and tied the knot, it became crystal clear we were meant for each other.

The life I lived while acquainted with Tyree had been a fucking roller coaster. I fell for two men only to help the main nigga kill the side nigga, what kind of BET movie type of shit is that? Never in years did I believe I'd be a victim all in the name of a four-letter word, LOVE! Tyree had my whole heart, and I had him without a doubt. He did any and everything for me. There was not one man who could take his place. That was until Xavier Cain Lyons was born, then he became my number one. I called him my love child because he was born on Valentine's Day.

As residents of Georgia, we were able to raise our son Xavier in a different environment. A violent neighborhood kept enemies, but our new location allowed us to blend into a suburban area. We lived the American dream that was mostly afforded to rich white folks. When I say we moved up like George and Weezie from *The Jeffersons*, you'd have to see it to believe it. Tyree purchased a million dollar home for the three of us to live in. All of the money he made from contracts continued to multiply until he finally decided to spend some of it.

I went from living in a comfortable condo to living like a celebrity in a privately gated six-bedroom, six-bath estate. Being a wife and mother made it seem as if life moved extremely fast. Despite the challenges, everything worked itself out as I learned the true meaning of being a multi-tasker. Through the body change and lack of sleep, my health remained well.

At times I did get homesick and missed my girl Keisha. Tyree grew fearful that I'd suffer from depression or post-partum. To prevent it, he provided me enough cash to sightsee a few days a week. I enjoyed the historic down-town, restaurants, and museums. Difficult to adjust to a new city, the options to explore were limitless. Excited to learn about Atlanta and all it had to offer, I choose a different location each time.

We'd settled in long enough to get a daily routine set, but driving had been a challenge. Traffic turned out to be the least favorite thing about living in another state. For at least the first few months, Uber became my best friend for getting around. I had never been one of those drivers who were good at knowing street names. Instead, landmarks were my way of giving directions. Once transportation got resolved, I had to find a doctor.

A never-ending search for a female doctor finally came to an end as Dr. Harris met my satisfaction. It had been time for another check-up. If only my mother could see me, all grown up with a child of my own. I stood and admired my new shape in the full-length mirror. My 34B breasts swelled up to a 36D, workouts kept my stomach snatched, and my ass plumped up. Xavier was a bit of a cock blocker who had mastered the art of waking up the minute the dick got good.

For two weeks straight Tyree stayed home, which gave me time to think and enjoy "me" time. Being a mother meant no time to myself. I also learned alone time was a thing of the past. Motherhood turned out to be nothing I ever imagined, but it was something that I wouldn't trade. It became such a habit to take fifty pictures a day. I stared at Xavier's little body while he slept, and any adorable moments caught on camera. The joys of being a parent outweighed shitty diapers, no sleep, and crying.

Naptime became my favorite part of the day because Xavier and I developed a pattern that made things easier. Each day my mom skills improved. I became a pro at washing, drying, and folding clothes all in one day. Other times my sweet angel refused to let me move from room to room without a fuss. Of course, the baby remained in chill mode when Tyree was around.

I adored their bonding moments. It also gave me a chance to hid for thirty minutes in my woman cave right outside of the main estate. It brought me quiet and peace of mind. I even explored the city bit by bit and found a nice food spot too. As a woman who continuously gave, it became very important to indulge in self-care as much as possible. Since Xavier came into the picture, I had to give up smoking due to breastfeeding.

One evening after exploring Georgia, I made it home in time to get a glimpse of Tyree folding clothes while the baby laid on a cushioned blanket near him. It was the sweetest moment of the two together. If it were a picture, the average person would've seen a man with his son, but to me, he was my hitta, my lover, my life.

Not working a typical nine to five job drove me crazy at times, but after a while, I enjoyed it. Tyree insisted being a stay at home mom would be enough of a task. He sure didn't lie, that baby kept my ass busy as the day is long. Most importantly, Xavier slept through the night, which was a blessing.

Tyree stepped foot through the door with exhaustion written all over his face. It was obvious that he hadn't slept in a few days by the puffiness under his eyes. It still drove me nuts that he trained himself to function in that manner. With a soft kiss to his forehead, he made it to the couch as his body gave way flopping down. I warmed up leftover shrimp scampi and Texas Roadhouse style garlic bread. On a wooden serving tray, I delivered his meal with a Miller Lite on the side. Catering to my man was something I know for sure my mother wouldn't approve of. Shit, sometimes it's hard to realize it myself. This nigga killed a man over me, so the least I could do was cook and treat him with love. There was no doubt our love for each other was real. It was all or nothing.

"Baby while you smash that I'm about to fill the tub and roll up."

"Come here for a second," he reached out for me holding my wrist glancing up into my face.

"Do you think I'm an evil person? Really, I do so much bad shit that it keeps from me sleeping at night."

I kneeled and stared at him.

"Tyree, we don't get to choose how some shit happens in our lives, but as an adult, we know right from wrong and action equals consequence. I guess what I'm saying is, I see good in you, past the dark side. Your life ain't been easy, so I'll never fully understand how you feel."

If anyone was to ask me did I see myself where I am now five years ago, the answer would be no. When I lost my mother, life changed unexpectedly, then out of nowhere, Tyree came along. Each day that led up to where we are now as husband and wife can be summarized as a blessing. We had a crazy, intoxicating type of love, a bond that could only be broken by death.

TYREE LYONS

Erika must have smiled for a week straight when we finally got settled into our renovated home. I made sure to have it gated, not to mention the pool right out back. Laps became a part of my twice a day routine. Our spot had so many rooms that we got walkie-talkies to keep in each room. Eventually, we made our mark to make it feel like home. I had never seen Erika glow and smile so much since we first met. I caught myself staring at her randomly wondering how she did what she did. She had been my personal angel, the one who had been sent to change me in ways I never thought. I often caught myself shaking my head in disbelief of the life I had built for myself and my family.

Once our son Xavier was born, Erika took my advice on being a stay at home mom despite her objections for part-time work. The transition from living single shifted to "we" and "our" type of conversations, something neither of us had been used to in the past. We had a few disagreements. However, parenting brought us even closer. We both agreed to give one another time alone each day in order to remain fresh. I never believed folks when they said you wouldn't get sleep after you have a child. Lucky for me, I had the gift to operate without sleep.

Secluded in my newly renovated man cave, I stared at the 50-inch plasma TV screen. Netflix and weed had become part of my routine whenever X slept through the night. I made the decision to cut back on traveling to spend quality time at home. Not traveling as often grew on me after a while.

Being a husband and father were two things I never knew would happen in my lifetime. There were many days I believed that my life would end the same way I took them. Religion hadn't been my cup of tea growing up, but I believed it must have been angels watching over Erika and me. Those gunshots could've ended Erika's life, as well as mine because she had become my life.

Living in the suburb of Georgia had many benefits for my family, most importantly, raising my son. Sure, we were no different from others, but I wanted him to have the same opportunity to grow up. Back in Milwaukee, so many young folks were killed and cheated out of life. I didn't want that shit for my son. Some nights I just stood and watched X sleep peacefully in his crib. Lord knows I feared him growing up to be a young black man. We lived in a time when the color of your skin got you killed by those who swore to protect and serve. Shit, nowadays, a fucking dog or gorilla will get more sympathy and airplay on the news over a young black shot down like a dog in the street.

⊏▭⊐

Each day that passed made me realize married life with Erika had been a beautiful thing. Commitment and trust were two things I found in her that changed my perspective.

Wiser with time, it truly dawned on me how important family was and what I missed out on as a child. Every moment spent with my son meant doing something positive, something that my bum sperm donor didn't do for me. Determined to make sure X had a better upbringing, he wouldn't want for shit. I set up a college trust fund for him that couldn't be touched until his high school graduation. Erika had an emergency fund as well, which I made accessible as needed in case death met me sooner than later. The more time I had to reflect and plan for my wife and child also made me grateful. So much so that I felt the need to write my boy a letter that he'd one day read.

Dear Son:

Until the day I met your mother, I never knew life could be so joyful, but then you were born. As your father, I promise to love you unconditionally and be there for you no matter the circumstances. You son, are my pride and joy. From this day until my demise, please know everything that I ever have done was for you and your mother. When you get older and finally open up this letter, I hope to still be alive to share the moment. In case I'm no longer alive in the physical sense, keep my words close. Never forget that each word is true. You son, have been the greatest blessing sent into my life during the toughest battle I had to face.

I'll always love you, my dear son, Xavier!

Love Pops

KENTRELL "MONEY" GIPSON

Living with two women and starting a family was nothing short of crazy, but I was willing to try. My love for Breya and Netta had been a complicated one. I wanted to be with both of them. Two kids added to the equation, and my mind went on overdrive. The promotion at work had been a great financial benefit. However, I needed more in order to care for two babies. During my lunch break, I browsed the internet for the fun of it and Googled "cost of raising a child" and damn near passed out. It reported roughly $12,000 within the first year, so imagine that number doubled.

I took any open shifts that came my way and all overtime in order to save up. Each check automatically deposited into two accounts. None of us had family around to help throw a baby shower or extend extra support. Therefore, we stacked our multiple incomes.

Fridays used to be my favorite day of the week because I had the weekends off, but going home grew draining. I couldn't keep up with the demands and meltdowns Breya and Netta had daily. At times, the girls went from friends turned enemies over shit like food or who got to spend more time with me. On the way inside the house, I stepped right into the drama. They were shouting back and forth at each other in the kitchen.

"Damn, why the hell do y'all gotta keep going at each other's throats? Y'all are killing me here."

"Well, she needs to learn not to touch what doesn't belong to her. I'm craving a fucking Snicker ice cream bar only to see they are gone!" Breya shouted.

"Dude, I bought three boxes. They're gone already?"

"I'm sorry," Netta sobbed. "I didn't eat all of them by myself, but I ate the last one. Sorry, not sorry."

"I guess yo' peanut head ass son wanted more," Breya blurted.

"Aye, you out of line now fall back!" I yelled.

Brea retreated, leaving Netta and me alone. She knew I was pissed at her for the petty antics. Facing Netta, I bent down, lifted her shirt, and kissed her round stomach as my hands gripped her ass.

"Hey, lil man! You already causing trouble," I teased. The second my lips pressed against Netta's stomach again, his little ass kicked me as if he understood me.

"Ha! Did you feel that, baby? He heard you. I need to sit down now," she mumbled and wobbled to the sofa.

I went to find Breya because we all had to coexist for the kid's sake. Ever since the women found out the sex of the babies, Breya turned into the baby mama from hell. Unhappy she couldn't give me a boy shattered her. Netta, on the other hand, was carrying my son, and that fueled Breya's hate. She purposely said and did petty shit to get under Netta's skin, but it only pissed me off.

Whenever she pissed me off, I went to the garage to burn a blunt and read the many baby books that I had stashed. Each puff got me to thinking deeper and deeper how loving two women at the same time resulted in babies.

The further along their pregnancies went, the more I learned about women and the entire pregnancy process. I definitely regret not wearing a condom. Don't get me wrong. My love for both women and children is real. I just wish it all happened differently. My world revolved around Breya and Netta, and it damn near drove me nuts, not to mention the doctor visits and nursery set-up.

As the delivery date drew near each of us tried to mentally and physically prepare the best we could. Breya and Netta were due around the same time, which meant we had to be ready for anything. Babies had a funny way of doing shit at the wrong time. We had double everything set up in the nursery. The only thing missing was the babies. As sure as shit stank, Breya and Netta's water broke at the same damn time. My ass didn't know if I was coming or going as I tried to get them and the bags into the truck. The ladies held on long enough for me to speed through two stoplights without incident before the foul language began.

"I can't believe I let yo' black ass knock me up?" Breya shouted at me.

"Shit, me either!" Netta yelled from the behind me. "This some straight bullshit. Nigga, keep your hands off me after this baby is out of me. I will be damned if this happens again."

I didn't pay either any attention because they never turned the dick down. Besides, women always said shit they didn't mean in the heat of the moment. By the time I sped through two more stoplights without incident, I was greeted with immediate assistance. The nurses were Johnny on the spot and gave me a chance to catch my breath.

In the same hospital next door to each other, I went back and forth between both rooms a few minutes at a time. With me being only one person, it grew exhausting. Breya had dilated to seven centimeters. I tried to spend more time in her room. Her contractions happened frequently and lasted longer and longer. Nervous, I watched the nurses prep, and it suddenly sunk in our daughter was almost here.

Netta, on the other hand, had remained in the first stage of labor and had yet to dilate more. In a way, it worked out perfectly because I was able to spend enough time with each woman.

"Breya, our daughter, is so beautiful!"

One look at her took my breath away, and life had forever changed. Heaven Denise Porter had stolen my heart. Breya held her for a few minutes before taping out in need of sleep.

"Get some rest, baby girl! I'll be next door," I assured her with a kiss to the forehead.

Just in time for part two, Netta had finally made progress and was about to push out my son. I stood proudly by her bedside while the doctor coached Baby Jayce out. Netta yelled a lot more than Breya, I assumed from the pain and pressure of his head. With front row seats, the visual of childbirth could never be unseen and had been engraved into my mind.

"Wow, you did it, baby! Our son is here!" I exclaimed proudly for the second time of the day.

"Oh my goodness, I'm really a mommy! Let me hold him," Netta requested. After the nurse cleaned and wrapped up Jayce, she placed him in her arms.

While Netta held Jayce, I retrieved my phone from my

back pocket and quickly set the video to record the special moment. A woman giving birth had to be the most beautiful gift a human could do with the body. Twice I witnessed why women are so strong and have for years have been the backbone of most families. In those minutes of capturing Netta and Jayce, I vowed to be better for them all.

━━━

Two days later, I returned to the hospital, anxious to get my family. I made sure the nursery was ready to welcome my babies. Breya and Netta talked about the food they wanted to eat upon returning home. Their every wish became my command. After witnessing each woman push out a bowling ball, they deserve the world. With assistance from a couple of the nurses, they helped get the women to the van. I carried Heaven and Jayce who lay snuggled in their car seats without a care in the world.

All I could do was stare at my son and daughter and smile with pride as they slept like angels. Their little chests rose up and down with each breath they took. I just wanted to watch them all night but needed a little shut-eye before work. As quiet as possible, I slipped out of the nursery and tiptoed to the bedroom. Behind closed doors, I found Breya and Netta both sitting with their big ass titties hanging out. Unable to resist my lips found their way to each breast.

"Get yo horny ass back. My nipples already sore from your greedy daughter," Breya ordered. She then hooked up the double breast pump and went to work.

"It feels good to me," Netta confessed.

"The shit tastes good too," I whispered as a squirt of milk hit my tongue. I moved over to the bed and stretched out while they did their business.

The women eventually got their act together, and shit kinda went back to normal. We tried hard each day to give space when needed to avoid arguments or blow-ups. Netta still held on to her apartment and even stayed there when she got tired of us. People on the outside looking in might think we're crazy as hell, but it's our lifestyle. The three of us raised our children and lived a life just as other families did.

THE END